T0162071

THE

Magician's Study

A GUIDED TOUR OF THE LIFE,

TIMES, AND MEMORABILIA OF

ROBERT "THE GREAT" ROUNCIVAL

Turtle Point Press

NEW YORK

The first three chapters ("The Inlaid Doors,"
"The Traveling Extravaganza," and "Letters to
Doughboy"), plus a small portion of "The Paper
Vaquero," appeared as "Letters to Doughboy" in
Things Magazine (U.K.), issue 17, in fall 2003.

Design and composition by Jeff Clark at
Wilsted & Taylor Publishing Services

FOR MOM, DAD, AND JAKE

For your love, understanding,

and all that patience

ONE

Life is short.

—P. T. Barnum, in a letter urging that the Barnum Museum of Natural History be built as quickly as possible.

THE
Inlaid Doors

Ladies and gentlemen. Good morning. Before we officially begin the tour, I would first like to ask all of you, *please* do not touch any of the objects in the room. I urge you to remember: this is not a tea-cozied library for the Forsythia Society, this is the study of Robert "The Great" Rouncival.

Also, please be so kind as to turn off any cell phones, pagers, or any other such beeping apparatus. We ask this not only as a courtesy to your fellow tour members, but also because certain elements of the study are extremely sensitive to sound and may react to such mechanical intrusions in unpredictable ways.

Before we open the doors—mahogany from darkest Africa inlaid with red marble quarried from a single, eight-foot bed located in the Italian Alps—a bit about Robert the Great. While I shall further explore, and perhaps even explain, the oddities of this great magician's life during the tour, a few essentials are necessary first.

Born on Midsummer's Eve in 1896, Robert James Rouncival was raised very close to this estate, in Kingston, New York. The son of a modest watch repairman named Thomas Rouncival and his wife, Elaine, Robert was an eager, curious child who loved to explore the farms and fields surrounding the town. At the age of ten, however, Robert suffered a severe mishap. During a summer excursion on a day perhaps as glorious as today, Rouncival crossed a pasture to go swimming in a nearby creek. Passing through a seemingly docile herd of Holstein cows, he was suddenly kicked and had his left leg broken very badly. A local sawbones botched the setting of the limb, and for the rest of his life Robert was hampered by a severe limp and terrible shooting pains up and down the leg. Perhaps the only saving grace of this injury was that it prevented him from service during the First World War. His younger brother William, only a year less in age, was not so fortunate.

Confined by the injury and later by the agony of the misset bone, Robert became a child of the indoors, watching and learning as his father repaired broken timepieces. From that point on, the inner-tickings, the construction, the setting and resetting of the bones, if you will, of the universe always fascinated him. This period may also have set Rouncival on his path towards misanthropic cynicism, as attempts to play with other youths were met with scorn and abuse. The children of his neighborhood called Rouncival "Hobble" and far worse, and he was forever bitter regarding the torrent of shame he endured at such an impressionable age. After one particularly disastrous outing, where the children first threw dirt clods at Rouncival and then chased him away while parodying his limp, Robert came home and told his mother, "They think they can mock me, but they see nothing. I shall show them!" Mrs. Rouncival was understandably upset at the vehemence of her son's feelings but there was little she could do to assuage his pain. With this in mind, that his entire career can be viewed as an act of vengeance perhaps as immature as the vitriol that inspired it, let us now enter the study.

THE

Traveling Extravaganza

Please, come forward, come forward. And would the last person through please shut the study doors? They, if anything, are safe to touch. My gratitude, young sir. Now, I understand that at first impression the study is hardly what anyone could expect. It should be said that the room was designed originally as an atrium, and thus the various tall windows and the high glass ceiling. It was during the early 1930s, when Rouncival permanently retired to this estate, that he converted the atrium into the shelf-lined study that is currently awing you. More on the construction of the study later, however. For now, let us look to the niche on your left, there along the short wall, containing the circus poster.

As I was saying, Rouncival grew up a child of the inside light, sitting at his father's elbow and brooding on his various abuses.

As a student, he showed a clear aptitude for mathematics and the sciences, while history and most of literature bored him to tears. Even as an adult, Rouncival read only as a matter of necessity, though he did take clear pleasure from the murderous conundrums offered by Misses Christie and Sayers. It was during such a period of dissatisfied quietude that Robert did as many alienated youth have only dreamed of doing: in early 1914, he fled home and joined the circus.

Before you imagine sequined acrobats, glamorous tents, tamed lions or mighty elephants, please know that this particular show hardly merited the title of "circus." Rather, it was a motley collection of aged and mangy animals, arthritic contortionists, not-so-strong men, and gimcrack tinkers. As you can see, the poster is shoddy print work indeed—whether that is a tiger in the upper right corner or merely a very strange goat has always baffled me—but it is the sole artifact Rouncival brought away from his years on the road. The show was called "Welt's Traveling Extravaganza," with the carnival run by a genial huckster named Barnabas Welt. A former clown of Vaudeville himself, Welt had a deep sympathy for circus folk, no matter how over-the-hill they may have been, and his circus was a veritable refuge for those that couldn't or wouldn't give up the life. It was fortunate for Rouncival that Welt was such a person, for who else would have taken on a lamed, spindly, penniless youth as a gofer and all-around assistant? Rouncival would always claim that Barnabas Welt was the kindest man he ever met, though this was said at times with a borderline sneer.

Thus, as the lamps of Europe were doused and the old world was murdered beneath the mud of Flanders, Robert Rouncival tramped the mill towns, logging camps, and farming communities of upstate New York and New England. From Blue Mountain in the Adirondacks to the rubbish-strewn lots of Worcester, Massachusetts to the hardscrabble hollows of Vermont, Robert acted as Welt's advance man. Limping into small villages and towns, he told everyone which rented-for-the-weekend field or empty warehouse the Extravaganza could be found at. It was probably during this time that Rouncival also acquired his taste for drink, as Welt, an abstainer, insisted that Robert tack a poster in every crossroad tavern or factory gin mill along the way. So Rouncival began to grow into a man, and a hard man at that, learning everything he could from the sad, faltering tricks of a dilapidated circus, its run-down folk, and its often impoverished audiences. And as he did so, he wrote to his brother William in the war.

Letters

TO

Doughboy

Now, I know you've all been standing for quite some time—yes, madam, your grimace gives away a slight air of discomfort—so why don't you all come this way and seat yourselves on the pillows and divans in the corner of the study Rouncival fancied "the Khan's tent." The carpets and wall hangings are all from Persia or beyond, with the one shading the window once a possession of a nineteenth-century Emir of Bokhara, the same cruel Emir who cast two Englishmen into a vermin-filled pit for years on end before finally having them beheaded in the center square. The Englishmen, it should be noted, were most definitely spies for the East India Company. Please feel free to pour yourselves iced tea from the service on the table there, itself a family heirloom of the Tsarist hero General Cherniaev, known in his time as "The Lion of Tashkent" for the conquest of that ancient bastion of the

Silk Road. Here in the study, you are always, always surrounded by wonders.

Is everyone all set? There are fresh lemon slices on that tray, yes madam, right there. Of course, take as many slices as you like. Ah, I see you are a great fan of lemon in your tea. You will, no doubt, be safe from scurvy into the foreseeable future. I am joking of course.

I will take this moment to loosen my tie. Already the heat of the day is affecting me, though the Khan's tent is certainly cool enough. Now, is everyone settled? Then I will continue. So, Robert tramped the wilds of the Northeast, learning all he could during his time with the Traveling Extravaganza. From the clowns he mastered tumbling, make-up, and crocodile tears, while the sleight-of-hand artists showed him how to conceal a card, or an automobile if need be, up his sleeve. The Extravaganza's sole artificer, a French-Canadian rummy styled "Babel the Brilliant," explained to Robert what he could of hidden contraptions and the mundane-unto-magical effects of smoke and mirrors, while Welt taught by example the purity of showmanship and a hearty slap on the back. Alongside these and many other things, Rouncival was also introduced to "The Plush Tent of the Tigress," a less-than-legal aspect of the show that Welt allowed at the dark, outer edges of the Extravaganza. It was in the tent of the Tigress, where Ruby Lily, Queen Serpentina, and Amazonia Snowdon plied their midnight trade, that Robert became a man.

You may ask: how do we know of Rouncival's strange compatriots? The answer is: from the many letters he sent to his younger brother William, who was away in the war. While Robert periodically wrote to his parents to assure them of his well-being, the notes were perfunctory at best; if he included any money to his financially strapped family, the letters made no mention of it. But to his brother, whom Robert referred to as "Doughboy" part in jest and part in bitterness for his own deformity, he told everything. William Rouncival himself had been equally unsatisfied with life in Kingston. Correctly foreseeing that America would have to abandon its isolationism and join the war, William enlisted in 1916. When America did indeed enter the conflict, William had already risen to the rank of lance corporal and was sent to Europe as part of the A.E.F. It was there, fighting in the trenches of France, that he received most of Robert's correspondences.

I have here, in what you see is a bloodstained packet, the letters, from which I will read a few short excerpts. William's end of the correspondence can only be guessed at, as Robert would set the letters adrift in the Gulf of Mexico shortly after the war. That he saved only his own words is typical of Rouncival's continuous self-reinvention. What the remaining notes do reveal is that both William and Robert were, despite their various hardships, still very much young men. Teenagers, if you will, both thrown into the heaving cauldron of the world at a very early age.

Surprisingly or not, the main subject of the correspondence was in fact their escapades with women. The grimmest, most horrific details of life on the road or at the front are related only in the shortest, most obtuse terms, while an intrigue with a willing mademoiselle behind the lines or a dalliance in the tent of the tigress received wide-eyed detail. Of course, we know William's side only from Robert's commentary, but still, certain themes are obvious. The following letter is distinct from the others for the amount of time spent describing a confrontation in a forlorn hamlet in upper New York. To wit:

Dear Doughboy,

Hah! That is what I must say most of the time. Every day, something new, like a blemish on the face, which puzzles me with its familiar, yet slightly different aspect.

We are in Fort Edward right now, and I must tell you, when you come home, should you find yourself in Fort Edward you will pray to return to the front or the back or wherever you are at this moment. The rats can be no bigger, the skies lower, or the people surlier. Being allowed to return fire only seems fair, as the residents are shooting glances right and left. While hanging posters at the tavern, twice I was called out by in-bred drunkards regarding my limp. Only the fortuitous entrance of Jerzy (in search as always of the dog's hair) saved me from a thrashing. How often can one believe that a Polish strongman will come to one's rescue? Not often, I think, and soon I shall begin to carry a cane (not that I need one) or a pistol to shut the louts up. As it was, Jerzy and I stayed on at the tavern for a while and took most of the patrons' coin with the Three Blind Men card game. (Have you been practicing? I tell you, master that and you will win all the cigarettes you could smoke in a lifetime!) In the meantime, if things get as rough as they did last week or whenever you last wrote, and don't tell me Black Jack has now forbidden pencils at the front, I'll send Jerzy your way. For a Pole, he's good in a pinch.

As you can tell, young Robert was already a bit of a cutthroat, a young man more than familiar with the rough ways of tavern folk. And advising William to cheat his mates of their rations? Sharp practice indeed. Here is another, more usual, type of note, written, we think (Robert never bothered to date his letters) in the late spring of 1918.

Doughboy,

   Oh, Doughboy Doughboy Doughboy! Have I one for you! You may be proud of pulling off that affaire (as you put it so daintily) the other day, and I do congratulate you on certain aspects: a redhead in the coop and a chicken for the company's cook pot afterwards is good work indeed! Birds in both hands, and the bar would stand you for the night on the story (if true) alone. But I must tell you, this morning I had quite the affaire myself. First, there was a near-catastrophe last evening. A farmer became enraged at Babel's chicanery, as apparently the watch had been of some value to the poor serf, and a riot near started. Welt, who should have seen it coming, had us off before the girls were even packed. So this morning I took the time to check if Amazonia was all right after our unseemly departure. I know, I know, I shouldn't go to see her so often, it puts me at times in a blue way, but this time, oh Doughboy, this time it was different. Perhaps it was because we have camped near a quiet little stream, the weather is surprisingly mild, and she had just come back from washing, but the usual hurried, ruttish way was absent. We laughed at the farmer of the night before, and as she sought something to wear, her trunks were in such disarray that the only thing she could find were her old gypsy scarves. She came from behind her curtain (a line of rain-gray rope tied from one end of the tent to the other with an old horse blanket slung across it) and seeing my expression, she gave the queerest smile and began to dance. It wasn't so much a dance as a waving, as though she became a rainbow breeze, and I gawked, stunned for a moment. Yes, I admit, "stunned" is the word and I am not ashamed to say so: it is only fair that a man of the world would gawk, slavering, at a mostly naked woman in a cloak of many colors. This did not last for long, however, and we were soon at it, doing things, doing such things,

Doughboy. I think perhaps she was infected with the stream or the mild sunlight, but it was something, and not something the rubes get for their two dollars in the Tigress either. Breasts that once seemed ponderous felt spry, if that is a good word for an aging fortune-teller's tits. The rest of her was spry as well, and ever since I have been as one clonked on the head, floating. I hoped writing would clear my mind but it seems to have done the exact opposite. I will go with her down to that stream at midnight tonight if I have to carry her myself. Ah, such an image: me limping (no, striding!), the great Amazonia over my shoulder under the moonlight, into the waters, all things a breeze. Hah!

In sadder news, poor Dozy seems to be on her last legs. Where Welt will find another camel is beyond me. Scranton by tomorrow night. Slay the Hun and join me, but stay away from the Amazon, she's mine! Love, Robert the Great

Obviously feeling good after his morning gymnastics, this is the first time Robert ever refers to himself as "the Great." Sadly for us, this is the final letter of the correspondence. William Rouncival was killed by a shell in the vicinity of Chateau Thierry during the last major German offensive of the war. The letters were sent to Robert's parents, who then gave them to Robert when he and the Extravaganza next passed through Kingston in September of 1918. He stayed up the entire night, reading his own words to a lost brother. The following morning he went to Welt and asked for his wages for the season. True to his benign nature, Welt paid the boy knowing full well Rouncival would use the funds to abandon the Extravaganza. As for Barnabas Welt, he soon felt his age and returned to his own people in the South, living the rest of his life at a family-owned tuberculosis sanatorium in the mountains outside of Asheville, North Carolina. Dying himself of T.B. within three years, Welt asked to be buried in full clown regalia, and his family obliged. Still somehow on her last legs, Dozy the camel was present at the funeral as the Traveling Extravaganza's sole representative.

Paper Vaquero

My word, look at the time. As usual, I have dawdled over the early part of Rouncival's life. If I have been overlong with these details, my apologies. Perhaps for my own reasons, this period of Robert the Great's life fascinates because it is so often overlooked, or at the least unexplored. Please leave your cups right there on the table, I shall take care of them later, and we will now enter the legendary period of Rouncival's life. Please follow me across the study to the long wall, where Robert kept his most treasured possessions. I know, I know, to forsake the comforts of the Khan's tent can be difficult, but nevertheless . . .

Young sir, please! Though it is dangerous only in its history, please do not spin that globe; it is a relic of Longwood, Napoleon's manor of final exile on the island of St. Helena. Thank you, yes,

I am relieved now. And you may have wondered about the tremendous number of books here in the study. As I told you before, Rouncival was notoriously lethargic regarding the written word. In fact, the volumes on these shelves are merely *trompe l'oeil* replicas. See, the library is hollow and the authors are entirely fictitious. As you may have heard, though, the wooden books are arranged in a deliberate order, and lexicographers, library scientists, even military code breakers, have studied the catalogue system in order to discover what, if any, secret the library contains. One gentleman, who if I may comment was in all aspects a madman, actually insisted the catalogue was a coded edition of one of the alchemist Maimonides' lost or supposedly burned treatises. To this I say only: doubtful. It is far more typical of Robert to have created a façade of false knowledge. Deploying such a disposable, and easily ascertained, trick was a weakness of his. It should be noted that examinations of the hollow volumes did reveal a number of papers, from both Rouncival and Margaret Tillinghast. During various periods of the study, both used the empty library as a repository of their more precious, or secret, correspondences. As I am sure you all know, Margaret Tillinghast—sole heiress to the Wampum Flour Company fortune, jazz baby, and occasional participant in Rouncival's escape artistries – was the woman who, in equal measures, contributed to the rise, then fall, of Rouncival's fame. There will assuredly be more on Ms. Tillinghast later in the tour.

Okay! What you see before you is a papier-mâché skeleton of the sort most often seen during the Mexican festival of the Day of the Dead. The hat and vest signify that this particular skeleton is meant to be that of a cowboy, or *vaquero*, if you will. Similar to the circus poster, this is the lone object kept by Rouncival during his second stage of wanderings. Crushed by the death of William,

Robert fled North America entirely in order to be alone with his sorrow and rage. This period of his life is perhaps the most mysterious of any portion, as Rouncival did not write to anyone, his parents included. What is known is that he used his final wages to book himself passage to the Caribbean and from there wandered the Latin American periphery. It is assumed that Rouncival used his conjuring skills to perform on the street and thus keep himself afloat but, again, very little is actually known. Rouncival kept the details of his sojourn a secret, saying only to a Chicago reporter one time, "It was a sordid land, filled with snarling, sordid people, and I was just another one of them, albeit with a limp and a very bad sunburn." It was during this time that legend says that Rouncival apprenticed with a Haitian voodoo doctor and learned many of the black arts in a hut on a jungle mountaintop. Obviously, no one will ever know the truth of this, though his skills in magic afterwards did seem to take on an unprecedented depth, a depth not easily explained.

The one concrete fact of Robert's days of exile is the meeting of his now almost equally famous personal assistant, Sherpa the Silent. Sherpa was in fact of Cuban heritage, a sailor and pirate of the Caribbean. Somewhere in his late twenties, he was really named Roberto Hernandez, and how he and Rouncival met was indeed sordid. Apparently, Robert found himself in a sinister confrontation in a waterfront tavern somewhere along the Yucatan coast, and for reasons unclear Hernandez used his own considerable knife skills to save Rouncival from a bloody death. Like the appearance of Jerzy the strongman earlier in life, Robert's good luck continued so far as bar room saviors was concerned.

Following their victory, Robert and Hernandez became fast friends, exploring the seedier elements of the Mexican coast together. At one point they even penetrated the thick jungle in order to find a temple of Mayan origin, which Robert in that same Chicago interview would describe as "the perfect conglomeration of God and creeping rot." As they traveled, they hit upon a scheme to further draw attention to Robert's street-side magic acts, and they concocted a story of Hernandez being of Tibetan stock, a lost lama seeking to return to his home on the roof of the world. So Hernandez became the usually silent Sherpa, standing hawk-eyed and hawk-nosed at Rouncival's right, hidden knife kept at the ready. When Sherpa did speak, he called the sandy-complexioned Rouncival *Sahib*, and did so with a gibbering accent again entirely concocted. No doubt, the two friends were laughing up their sleeves the whole time. Clothed in a wild amalgamation of gypsy, horse thief, and voodoo priest, they proved such a success in the plazas that Rouncival proposed they go to America to try their act there amidst the monied frenzy of the burgeoning Jazz Age. With little else to do aside from drinking, fighting, or pirating, Sherpa agreed readily.

They left during the festival of the Dead, and that is when Robert brought back the one souvenir of his days of sordidness. The paper skeleton was long a small aspect of his stage show, kept in the background as a kind of glum motif. The beautiful necklace around the neck and the arrows you see embedded in the ribs are later additions. Apparently, during a party in the study in the mid-1930s, Rouncival and the artist Frida Kahlo became so inebriated that they practiced their archery at the poor vaquero. The blood-red spot in the region of the heart is from her palette, and the hand-painted serpent beads were given to the vaquero directly from Kahlo's own throat. For this alone, the dead vaquero has been valued as priceless despite being a rather cheap souvenir of its time. Fakir that he was, Rouncival would have enjoyed this estimation quite heartily.

THE

Orphan Timepiece

Just a short walk now, thankfully far less than Robert's return to America. Though we don't have time, you see there that framed newspaper print? It is from a now-defunct New York daily and the first-ever review of Robert's show. It is a pan, and Robert, perhaps infected with the hot temper of the Latin world, challenged the reporter to a duel in Central Park's Sheep Meadow. Luckily for Robert, the newspaperman did not appear at the scheduled appointment. Most assuredly, the intrepid reporter would have perished in that meadow, either by Robert's hand or, more likely, by Sherpa's.

But before Robert's act can receive its first poor mention, it must take the stage, and that took a bit of doing. Rouncival and Sherpa, perhaps through one of Sherpa's old Caribbean acquaintances, returned to America via the seas, arriving at New York Harbor in May of 1921. Disgusted with Prohibition, as well supposedly with the success of the women's suffrage movement, Robert wished to see his home and family. Taking a Spanish molasses barge up the Hudson River, which Robert later claimed was called *The Dolorosa*, the friends arrived at Kingston only to discover the death of Robert's mother, Elaine Rouncival. In his absence, she had died during the Spanish influenza epidemic. It was Robert's second funereal homecoming in as many trips, and the effect upon him was grim. Though gladdened to see his father, Robert took to the taverns yet again for an extended period, Sherpa at his side, and the summer was spent in hollow-chested debauchery. They did assist Mr. Rouncival, whose eyesight was failing quickly, with his watch repairs, which Sherpa was fascinated by.

On the whole, however, the return to Kingston was a disaster. Unable to give up their rough, waterfront ways, Robert and Sherpa could be found most evenings in the illegal saloons around the riverside Roundout area of town. There, as usual, they drank and brawled, with the Kingston toughs taking no degree of delight in picking quarrels with Sherpa. The town's distrust of the two wild foreigners—and make no mistake: Robert was by now a very foreign entity—was such that he and Sherpa were regarded as thieves, Bolsheviks, homosexuals, or a combination of all three. That the young women of the village found the two wild men enticing only exasperated matters with the local ruffians. Even dour Robert realized the situation was untenable, and by late October he told his father they were off again, this time to New York City. He'd been practicing various routines with Sherpa and felt it was time to make their fortune.

The evening before their departure, Thomas Rouncival presented his son with a gift: a pocket watch and fob made entirely from used, discarded, or otherwise orphaned parts accumulated throughout the years. Robert called the watch "my most hideous, tormented, treasured possession," and it can be found right here, in my vest pocket. As you can see, it is indeed a timepiece of odd appearance, though most skillfully made. What you cannot see is that inscribed upon the back are the simple words, *For My Son*. Thomas Rouncival, who'd also given Sherpa a small folding pouch of watch-repairing tools, died of pneumonia in February the following year. When he received the news, Robert told Sherpa, "Going home to yet another death will kill me as well." Robert did not return to Kingston for the funeral, or ever again for that matter, and he immediately sold the house and the shop at the back, his entire inheritance, for far less than its worth.

THE
Silver Stage

Ah, madam, I see the grimace has returned. Though it has been said I appear young for my age, I too am beginning to glance longingly towards the benches and small stage at the center of the study. Let us approximate Robert's zig-zag path through life and head that way. If you all would be so good to excuse a momentary informality, I shall seat myself at the lip of the stage. So much better. Please rest on the benches and let us take just a second to ponder a typically overlooked aspect of Rouncival's life. As we are already feeling strained from our standing and shuffling, imagine then how Rouncival must have suffered during his lengthy performances. The pains in his leg often made the act an ordeal. In fact, madam, and do excuse my referencing the lemons again, no insult is intended, Robert insisted that the juice of a citrus fruit relieved the pains in his joints. After more than one performance, he could be found in his dressing area, leg bared, with a cut-and-squeezed lemon perched atop his kneecap. Ha, I am glad to see the grimace has transformed to mirth. I too am tick-led every time I consider Robert the Great greeting his admirers backstage with a lemon on his leg.

While we shall abstain from such measures, nevertheless, to be seated is a relief. That we are seated upon or in front of the first stage of Robert the Great's career makes such relief that much more intriguing. In fact, these obviously charred boards and one-time stage for a Yiddish theater troupe are the true beginnings of Robert's greatness.

Rouncival and Sherpa arrived in New York City by late Octo-ber, 1921. With little funds saved from their wasted summer, they shared a room in a run-down hotel in the only neighborhood they could afford: the Bowery. Though perhaps not quite as fearsome as during its heyday at the turn of the century, the Bowery and the neighboring Tenderloin and Five Points districts remained slums of the worst sort. Prostitutes, cutthroats, thugs, thieves, cheats, sharps, pimps, addicts, gangs, the wanton, wicked, and unwanted all continued to make the Bowery their home. First-or second-generation immigrants were often thrown into this sinkhole of vice, and joining them out of necessity were Robert and Sherpa. That they did not become common criminals, petty pilferers, or die in a useless drunken orgy is testimony to Robert's powerful will.

Their residence, if it could be called that, was named the Half-Shell Palace. Located along lower 6th Avenue in the nether re-gion between the Bowery and the Tenderloin, the three-story Half-Shell had once been an oyster bar, with the owners living above. But when Robert and Sherpa entered the establishment seeking a cheap meal, they discovered that the Half-Shell Palace was actually a hotel, and one barely hovering above flophouse status at that. The owner of the Palace was a second-generation

German Jew named Bill Silver, actual name Wilhelm Zylbar. A runner and general fixer for the Tammany political machine, Silver had worked in various, discreet roles for both Big and Little Tim Sullivan. With the death of Little Tim in 1913—he died, like Big Tim before him, a raving madman—Silver then did odd chores for the local bosses before deciding that he needed to retire from the faltering Tammany rackets. Silver purchased the unused Half-Shell in 1915, converted it into a hotel, and made a solid if not extravagant living by renting rooms to whoever staggered through the saloon-style doors. Any and all who stayed at the Half-Shell Palace remembered less than fondly the intensely cold lobby, where Silver and his Irish wife Maud sat huddled behind the oyster bar/check-in counter with a small coal stove warming their feet. Considering Rouncival's career, walking into the Half-Shell seeking a dinner and finding instead Silver hunched behind the grungy hotel counter can be seen in hindsight as Fate furiously weaving her webs.

For you see, behind the hotel, a small carriage house was located amidst the tenements of the neighborhood. Attainable only by way of a dim alley alongside the hotel, the carriage house itself had been unused for years. Inspired, Silver purchased it along with the Half-Shell, blacked out the windows, built a rough stage and a small riser in the back, then installed some benches up front and opened a theater named, in mockery of the movies he so detested, the Silver Stage. There, at least once a week, a small company calling themselves the Minsk Troupe performed the great dramas of the Yiddish theater. It was upon those very benches, watching the passion plays of the Hebraic faith, that Robert underwent his final apprenticeship. It was also at the foot of the Silver Stage that he fell in love for the first time, with none other than the cat-eyed chanteuse of the company, Roza Ellstein.

If you would, permit me a moment to set the stage. The conjunction of personalities, heritage, and aspirations alone is remarkable, though perhaps not atypical of the Bowery of the early 1920s. All roads met at the Half-Shell Palace that winter. We have Silver, former cog of the Tammany machine, with his shanty-Irish wife Maud, a morose, mostly silent personality who possessed a savant-like ability to replay any tune on the piano. Strange Maud often assisted the Minsk Troupe with their musical numbers, while Silver, despite owning an establishment named for shellfish, remained faithful to his Hebraic roots by allowing an amateur theater company to perform Yiddish dramas in his carriage house auditorium. Then we have young Robert and Sherpa, two roustabouts essentially at loose ends, performing in the street again for pennies, kept above a truly criminal existence only by Robert's burning, yet still confused, desires to become an artificer of real worth. Then add the Minsk Troupe to the tableau, led by a talentless writer and producer named Jacob Davidoff who happened to luck into one of the premier talents of her time, Miss Roza Ellstein.

A Jewess of German-Polish lineage, Ellstein possessed a rapturous alto voice and multi-colored eyes; her right iris was a lush green while the left was a far lighter, pale amber hue. To have seen Miss Ellstein, one week a dark and vengeful Lilith, the next a tormented victim of a savage dybbuk (a kind of ghostly, ghastly demon in Jewish folklore), only to return the following performance as Judith carrying the severed head of Holofernes, was to have witnessed a marvel. Just approaching her twentieth year and close to six feet tall, with mahogany hair and a voluptuous figure, it is no wonder Roza Ellstein alone rose above the Minsk company, becoming by 1923 a lead player with the legendary Folksbeine Troupe. That Rouncival, Sherpa, and Ellstein—

names of notoriety all—could all three come together if only briefly at such a distinct place and time proves: the distance from half-shell flophouse to the greater, silver stages of the world may be only a short stroll down a dank alley. Such is, or was, America.

I have rhapsodized enough. Let us return to the story, which was by the holiday season of 1921 very cold. Unused to such weather, Sherpa was extremely hard-pressed by the chill, and he took to wearing all of his costumes at once just to keep warm. With the robes, kaftans, headdresses, and whatever other flim-flam Robert told him to wear, he must have truly begun to look the part of a beleaguered Tibetan mountaineer. In fact, their act was hardly supporting them, and Robert took for a while (though he denied it later) to working what we would now recognize as an early form of a shell game. Never an obvious aspect of the con, Sherpa would lurk around, carefully observing Robert's gulls. At any hint of violence or wrath on their part, he would leap in pretending to be yet another victim of Rouncival's scams. With much clattering and shouting, Robert would allow himself to be chased down the street and around the corner by the maniacal, knife-wielding Sherpa. As an escape method, it was highly effective, but it also meant the two were forced to go further and further afield into bitter weather lest any previous witnesses see a repeat performance.

All in all, they were often down to their last nickel and took to spending their time in the lobby of the Palace, chatting with Silver and assisting him with whatever sots fell through the saloon doors seeking "berths," as Silver wryly referred to his beds. "The sooner we get them into their berths, the sooner they stop screaming" was the old man's mantra. The veteran of many a Bowery donnybrook, Silver enjoyed the young charlatans, realizing quickly they were relatively harmless, and he would often regale them with stories of the old neighborhood and its horrors. He relished telling of McGurk's Suicide Hall, where patrons took to tossing back carbolic acid in order to end their earthly misery; the Haymarket Dance Hall, so popular during its glory that the owner dared to charge an unheard-of-before admission price and actually got rich doing so, and Honest John Kelly's, a 24-hour gambling den whose Stygian doorman was nicknamed Dandy Jack. These stories entranced Rouncival, and Suicide Hall especially would become a notable aspect of his later, mystery performances. Still, a good story could only be so warming, and it was during a particularly freezing evening that Silver suggested the two young men attend a show by the Minsk Troupe, if only for the wealth of warm bodies in the carriage house.

While Robert had shown little interest in the comings-and-goings of the troupe, and he certainly did not have even a smattering of Yiddish, the night was so chilly that he and Sherpa pounced at Silver's suggestion. I have here Robert's description of first seeing Roza Ellstein as she performed in Davidoff's paltry revision of "The Golem." The description actually comes from a rare speech given by Robert himself to a meeting of the Harbingers' Club held right here in the study. And yes, madam, your smirk has given you away. Rest assured, there will be far more regarding the infamous Harbingers' Club before the tour is over. For now, let us content ourselves with Robert's entranced memory of that night, transcribed by the secretary of the club and later approved by Rouncival as an addendum to the official minutes, all of which were found within the hollow volumes.

My god, it was cold that night. The water bucket in our room had frozen over, and even standing down in the lobby with crazy Maud and the stove wasn't much help. Silver had gone out to find anyone passed out in the vicinity, as they certainly would not have survived the night. I was leaning on the counter, hoping against hope Maud would make some tea to take the chill off, while Sherpa just stood around by the stairs at the far end of the check-in, moaning and shivering beneath his bundles of rags. All I could see was his sharp, red nose sticking out from between the scarves.

Finally Silver reappeared, banging his way through those goddamn saloon doors, stamping and clapping his hands. He hardly gave Sherpa or me a glance as he darted behind the counter and then, so help me god, pulled down his pants in order to warm his bum by the stove. He stood so close I thought for a moment he was going to come to terrible harm but he seemed to know what he was about. As his behind heated, so did his ability to speak, and he and Maud began to get into their usual argument, though it was Silver that did all the shouting, about her cat.

You see, Maud had this old cat, a fat black thing she called Bear who she would set on the counter every now and then as if producing a magical treasure. Bear was pretty old and mostly slept next to the stove, winter or summer, all day and night long. But when he was on display, oh, how that kitty enjoyed it, and he had the oddest habit of ramming people with his head. It was Bear's way of saying hello and we all liked him well enough, but not the way Maud did. Every time she hefted that beast onto the counter, she would nod with absolute pride, "Bear comes from the Old World." This never failed to set Silver off. He would pound his fist, shout, holler, and generally make an ass of himself (which as you know he was hardly ashamed of in the first place), insisting that Maud stop lying about her cat. "You know good and well that cat is not from the Old World. Staten Island, maybe! Blarney County or wherever your people come from? No no no, that is impossible!" This hardly fazed Maud, who would just repeat stubbornly, "Bear comes from the Old World," with old Bear all the while lowering his head and bonking everyone in sight just to punctuate her point. Ah, but it was a gas to witness.

That night, however, it was too cold even to enjoy the usual display, and I think Bear just wanted to return to his nest by the stove. After Silver had settled himself down and gotten his behind pretty well roasted, he pulled his pants back up, gave Sherpa and me a squint, and said, "You fellows are making me cold again just looking at you. What, have all the bars in the Bowery closed for the winter?" Sherpa was shivering too hard to answer, while I just glared at the saloon doors and made a face. Silver didn't care, giving his usual excuse: "This is America, land of the cowboy, land of the free." I wanted to lasso him and tie him to a train track at that moment, but then Silver suddenly slapped the counter and said, "I know what you boys should do! The Minsk is playing at the carriage house tonight. It's a good one too, 'The Golem.' If that schmuck Davidoff doesn't ruin it, that is. Come along."

Sherpa and I barely budged. The poor Cubano was frozen to the stair railing, I think, while I hardly wanted to see a play in a foreign language in some horse barn down at the end of a rat-infested alley. Silver had put his coat and ridiculous Russian hat back on and looked like a bear himself, but he was halfway to the doors before he noticed neither of us were following him. He turned, whistled, and said again, "Come along. It will be warm. What else can anyone do in this cold?" Neither of us was convinced, and with a sigh, Silver surrendered and said the one thing that was guaranteed to rouse us: "There will be women there. Actresses. A good Jewess may be a good Jewess, but an actress is an actress also. I'll introduce you afterwards."

We were halfway down the alley, booting rats out of the way and pulling our hats lower, as Silver explained the play. "A golem is like a puppet, a puppet without strings but with the name of god under its tongue. Golems used to be created all the time by wizards too lazy to do chores, too poor to afford help, or too ugly to find a wife. Good to be a wizard, eh? Maybe that damned cat is a golem? More like a wizard he is. Hmmmm."

As Silver pondered the kabalistic secrets of Bear, we reached the end of the alley, where it opened into a small, cobblestoned square of sorts. The tenements blocked the whole area off, and the way they loomed above, a few lit windows, mostly dark ones, a few voices or cries falling down upon us, it felt as if we were at the very bottom of the world. We could hear the crowd chattering inside the carriage house, the usual buzz of neighbors meeting, greeting, and gossiping, while a lank man all in black stood huddled inside the doorway. Silver bustled all of us inside—"These are my friends, Adler, no charge. Good man, good man"—and like everyone else, we shuffled towards the big wood stove along the back wall. I wondered if Silver would bare his ass again, but he was too busy chatting up everyone to bother. It seemed so familiar, yet so different, to be in the playhouse. I felt the old rush of the Extravaganza surging in my veins, but with the foreign tongues and accents and clothes, it felt also so wonderfully alien. Also, so wonderfully warm. Sherpa was just beginning to unwind himself from his layers, and I could still hear Silver bemoaning Maud's lunacy, when the lamps were dimmed and the curtain rose. I expected to see some kind of evil sorcerer lazing about a castle chamber or maybe his puppet monster, but instead, I saw Roza Ellstein for the first time. She was dusting a mantle. As she dusted, she sang to an accompanying violin from behind the back-

drop, and I have never heard such a voice before or since. The richness, the quiet joy (she was obviously playing some kind of contented wife), everything seemed not so much a song of the voice but a sound emanating from her whole body. I could have sworn her fingers themselves let loose in song as she dusted. I couldn't comprehend a single syllable, but I understood everything. Or thought I did, until she turned and faced the audience. It was then that her two amber-then-green eyes played across all of us. I could feel Sherpa stiffen next to me, and I knew, knew, I was truly at the bottom of the world, and above the earth itself was the woman on stage, seeing all in multiple hues as she dusted a mantle piece with singing fingers.

I hardly remember the rest of the performance or the other performers either. There was of course the monster, played later I found out by Davidoff, and performed so stiffly and horribly it almost made for a good effect. I didn't then know the real play, and whatever inventions or distortions the writer had made were beyond me. Silver would often hiss at one of Davidoff's grosser translations, "Idiot! The man is an idiot," but I didn't care. How could I? I stared at the housewife, at her eyes, and I could tell once and once only she met me with her own eyes and knew I was a stranger to the carriage house, to her world. Of course, there was no blinding flash, at least for her at the moment, and she stayed in character, but I knew. The benches were filled that night, but I stood, I stood for the entire performance, and it was only when the curtain fell, blocking the wife from my sight, that I felt my leg about to buckle. I grabbed poor Silver's shoulder pretty hard as I struggled to remain standing and applaud at the same time, then I fairly shouted in his ear, "You must introduce us. You must." He smiled, nodded, then looked up and saw my expression, and his whole demeanor shifted, becoming very intent *and businesslike. Silver understood it was a matter of serious-ness, of matchmaking, even, and told me quietly with a pat on the hand, "Of course. But first, please stop breaking my arm."*

Ah-hah, and thank you: I too have felt like applauding at the conclusion of Robert's account. Though Robert, in his later years, may well have been waxing eloquent to the Harbingers' Club, that he stood for the entire performance was nigh on a feat. H. Leivick's "The Golem," first published in 1921, ran upwards of four hours! Of course, especially considering Rouncival's description of the opening scene, which differs completely from Leivick's poetic script, the golem he witnessed may very well have been the creation of another, now entirely forgotten author. The production could also have been simply, as Silver seemed to believe, the victim of Davidoff's incompetent direction. For the sake of our own sanity, let us drop any such conjectures and know only that, yes, Robert was instantly enchanted by Roza Ellstein, and enchanted to such an extent that he collapsed when the curtain finally separated him from the wife on stage.

A
Top Hat
ON THE
Doorknob

While we are not yet ready ourselves to leave the Silver Stage behind, please allow me to retrieve a prop before I continue with
Robert and Roza's soon-to-blossom romance. You no doubt have
noticed the top hat hanging from the closet handle here. The
closet actually contains many of Sherpa's later, magnificent costumes. Though some are quite extraordinary, we simply don't
have the time now to display them.

So, you see, an ordinary top hat, often worn by amateur magicians at children's parties, small fairs, and so on. And yes, young
sir, it is very much a laughing matter, whether perched on my
head or crowning another's. Rouncival felt the same way, despis-

ing it and the ubiquitous wand so many of his fellow artificers displayed on stage. Robert never actually wore this hat except in jest, but it was very much a part of his life. First, it served as the catch for whatever coins were thrown his way during the street performances, and second, whenever Robert or Sherpa was occupied with a young lady in their room at the Half-Shell, the top hat was hung on the outer doorknob so the other would know to leave the berth undisturbed. Perhaps the effect was magical-unto-mundane, but as a signal the top hat did the trick. Indeed, it became a running joke between the friends that to have a liaison with a young miss was to "pull the rabbit from the hat."

While they certainly had had their share of sexual experiences, it must be said that both Rouncival and Sherpa were at that time far more used to affairs with, how shall I say it, women of low birth. Pulling the rabbit from the hat more often than not involved a dance hall gin bout or even perhaps an exchange of coin. This makes them distinctive in neither their time nor their age group, but it does make Robert's desire to court Roza Ellstein an entirely new ball game, so to speak. Though she too was of middling-to-impoverished origins, and was as I mentioned even younger that the two rascals lurking at the Palace check-in, nevertheless she was most definitely a woman of far higher caliber than Robert had ever dared pursue before. That she was a Jewess, and often shadowed by the equally smitten Davidoff, did not help matters. It would have been extremely easy for Rouncival to abandon his hopes, especially considering the repugnance he felt for his twisted left limb, but something had changed within Robert. Whether it was Ellstein's enchantments or a newfound realization that he could stand for any amount of time given the proper circumstances (or illusion), Robert's desire to become a magician of fame and to have Roza combined into a single goal, a goal that he pursued with previously unseen diligence.

True to his word, Silver introduced Rouncival to Ellstein following the show, and Rouncival apparently rose to the occasion, making quite a good impression upon Roza. He also stated later that he more than embellished his role with the Traveling Extravaganza, claiming that he was the carnival's magician and not its gofer. As one would know from the legend of the golem, perhaps putting the correct word under the tongue is all that's needed to animate. By proclaiming himself a true artificer, Rouncival may well have become one at that moment, and directly in front of Ellstein's lovely multi-colored eyes to boot. As a brief aside, Robert would later say that was why he billed himself as "The Great": "If I say I am great, the audience, catcalls at hand, will probably hope to see that I am not, but the mere suggestion makes actual greatness possible. That is why no performer, ever, has dubbed themselves 'The Adequate.'"

With a combination of wheedling, boasting, and Silver's bemused compliance, Robert managed to get himself insinuated at the carriage house as a magic act. He and Sherpa began to open for the Minsk Troupe as a warm-up. While Davidoff, a sour personality at best, wasn't especially pleased to see any more of Robert's presence—he had taken to attending every one of the company productions, sitting front and center and no doubt gazing non-stop at the also bemused, yet charmed, Ellstein—Robert's sheer pluck was a hit with the audience. The weekly gate at the carriage house doubled as more and more came to see the fresh-faced conjuror and his silent, supposedly Tibetan assistant. That his act, with the dead vaquero brought down from the berth to the stage, was so seemingly at odds with the typically moralistic dramas of the Yiddish theater only seemed to enhance each show's effect. Rouncival, in love with his own, newly invented abilities, became a magician of startling confidence. He told shaggy dog stories, teased and taunted the audience, and loosed his illusions so casually that by the time the audience realized he had transformed a chair into a burning candle, they'd explode into applause even as the candle floated away into the rafters. One of his running gags was that he was scared witless of Sherpa, pointing at the dead vaquero with a shaking finger as though that had been the last man to cross the sinister Tibetan. Certainly he had more than a few flubs—his early attempts at ventriloquism failed badly, though later he would master that art to a terrifying degree—but his will was strong. If a joke or an illusion flopped, Robert would ignore the stillness and toss off yet another one-liner to break the silence. All in all, his youth, Welt-ian flourishes, fiendish energy, and simple ability to make objects disappear astonished the audience nightly. It should also be noted that Sherpa's previous experience constructing pirate hideaways was an invaluable help; by the time Sherpa had completed his adjustments to the stage, Rouncival would smirk, Hannibal's army of elephants could have been hidden beneath there.

Such were matters as winter progressed and the New Year, 1922, was rung in. Robert began to perform on his own one night a week on Saturdays, and while Silver took half of every show's gate, still, Rouncival and Sherpa had at least a bit of pocket money. Soon, it was Ellstein, escaping from the Sabbath dinner at her aunt's house, who could be seen seated on the front bench as Robert performed his routines. It was obvious to all that a romance was budding.

But then, in February, Rouncival received word that his father had died. It was Silver who handed Robert the telegram and Silver also who watched the silent Rouncival slowly limp up the

Palace stairs seeking his berth. The top hat was placed on the doorknob, and for two days Robert remained in his berth, alone. Though Sherpa knocked, Rouncival never answered. Finally, Robert emerged. He came down the stairs as slowly as he had mounted them, took Silver's arm, and said, "I need help. I want to sell my father's house. Now." Silver tried to intervene, pleading with Rouncival not to rid himself of the inheritance, but it was to no avail. Rouncival was determined to have nothing to do with his past. Stating his categorical objection to the entire matter, Silver then brought Rouncival to a shyster attorney, who had the place sold well under market value within two weeks. At the signing, Silver could only sigh with resignation, "Well, I suppose every young man must piss away at least one inheritance in his lifetime." Determined indeed to flush his new assets away, that night Robert took Sherpa, Silver, Ellstein, and Davidoff out for a night on the Bowery. The intention was to paint the town red, and by the end of the evening, Ellstein found herself in Rouncival's arms. Here, taken also from his lecture to the Harbingers' Club, is Robert's account of that wild night.

Before I begin, I would like to add that now is perhaps an appropriate time for the young gentleman to take a moment to wash his hands. Rouncival's account contains some explicit descriptions of his liaison with Ellstein. The young sir will stay? Ah, but it is good to see parents unafraid to allow their children at least a brief glimpse into the pleasures of the adult world. I am sure the young master will also, by the end of Robert's account, be a fervent admirer of Roza Ellstein.

What can I say of that evening? My father dead, my home sold, a roll of bills in my pocket, dressed in a new black shirt, collar, and coat, that beastly watch ticking solemnly next to my heart as we gathered in the lobby of the Half-Shell. Silver demanded that I give him at least half the money roll for safekeeping, but I'd have none of it. Sherpa too was duded up, though where he'd gone to purchase that crimson silk shirt was beyond me. He'd trimmed his moustache and beard down into an empire, and for the first time since the Yucatan he truly looked the swashbuckler. Silver, a dowd as always, wore black in honor of my father, though he brandished a wonderful hip flask before we went to fetch Roza. He displayed the inscription, "Bill Silver, for 20 Years of Valued Service, 'Little' Tim Sullivan," and we all sipped, in memory of Tammany's greatness and my father the watch repairman. Then we went out into the Bowery.

It was a short stroll up 6th Avenue to Roza's aunt's house. It was late February, starting to become dark, though an unseasonable thaw had enmeshed the city, and everyone was out on the streets, breathing air that didn't ice the lungs for the first time in months. Roza too was on her stoop, wearing a long fawn overcoat I'd never seen her wear before and shadowed as always by that fool Davidoff. The cashmere hung beautifully on her tall frame, and with those eyes, my god those eyes, gazing carefully at me from beneath what looked also like a new cloche hat, I could barely stand to look at her. I thought my chest would implode. I shook Davidoff's hand, a fishy grip if ever one existed, then inhaled deeply as Roza embraced me, whispering, "I am so sorry, Robert . . ." She smelled of violets or some such flower, she smelled like spring. Then she looked at me closely, holding me a moment at arm's length, and smiled. "Whiskey?" she asked, for let us not forget that Prohibition was nominally in place. Caught out as we were, I could only grin. With a charm I'd hardly ever seen him display, Silver reproduced the flask with a bow, and Roza and Davidoff also imbibed, both uttering a Hebrew toast, perhaps prayer for the dead, as they did so. With a wave to Roza's aunt lurking in an upstairs window, we were off.

If you've ever been on a carnival thrill ride at Coney Island or some such place, you will then know how that evening felt. Everything a blur, everything in motion, shouts, screams, open mouths, then the occasional stillness that has such import it becomes burned into the memory from amidst the maelstrom. Such was that night. Miracles, marvels, and many other things besides as we celebrated my newfound fortune. Down 6th Avenue we went, and down into some foreign, almost infernal, world we descended. I wish I could relate more of the night, but with so much a haze, again, it is only the marvels that stand out.

It began at Duffy's Point, perhaps the most decent establishment we would venture into the entire night. Silver passed the flask, glasses were raised, and the minstrels, a bunch of Irish waifs, struck the first chords. From there, already with a gaggle of drunken followers, we went to the Paladin, where Davidoff's impatience for drinks made the barkeep so irate that he flicked beer foam into Davidoff's shocked face. From there to the Gashouse where a man referred to Sherpa as a nigger and had his nose broken for his efforts while Sherpa somehow didn't even get a speck of blood or gristle on his shirt. On for a quick sup at a chinaman's chophouse before reaching the underground gin mill the Copper Penny, where a scaly eye peered at us through the peephole. It was only at the Penny that we paused, Silver taking Roza's arm quickly as he solemnly informed her, "This is not a place for ladies." Roza laughed and such a laugh it was, head thrown back with the deepness from her strong throat, those green and amber *eyes flashing. "Since when has an actress been considered a lady?" she smirked, grabbing the flask from his coat. Drinking heartily, Roza pounded the door directly beneath the watchman's eye and all together we reeled inside.*

The Penny was bedlam, and we were yet another group of inmates taking charge of the asylum. The throngs pressed back and forth from the bar to the dance floor, and Sherpa's beautiful crimson shirt the only way of maintaining a bearing as we waded in.

Somehow Silver found us a snug near the back (the man had a talent, a genius in fact, for such things) and we piled in, Roza positively hot against my shoulder as she stripped off the cashmere and reached for glasses. Toasts, more toasts, more toasts again, and Sherpa in red was on the dance floor, stepping lightly from one bird to another as his fancy dictated, a small, reeking cigar burning continuously from the corner of his mouth. Silver, like always, had discovered an acquaintance from his Tammany days and was plotting the downfall of the reformers who'd taken over City Hall. Roza in the heat took off her hat and let her dark, dark hair hang loose. With a cry, she too was out on the dance floor, next to Sherpa, and together, well, together they burned the dance floor down. Even amidst the uncouth floods, space cleared for them to cut the rug. God knows what those steps actually were, and I, with my leg and all, hardly knew whether they were doing the Turkey Trot, the Collegiate Shag, or the Charleston, thankfully a craze just then in its infancy. I must admit, for a time I felt a pitiable, self-pitying envy for Sherpa, understanding for the first time Davidoff's equally pitiable predicament. He was almost comatose from all the drink, and though I felt nothing but scorn at the time, he could hardly be blamed for falling out. Remember: accustomed more to the frolics of coffee house malin-

gerers, he was hardly in his element with a former carnie, a La-tino pirate, and a hardened Tammany man. Even now I can hardly think of a group better suited to heavy indulgence. Still, I too was a bit worse for the wear at the moment, and let my sod-den mind wander for a time. Then coming back up, I saw Roza and Sherpa standing in front of the table. My expression must have given me away, for Roza turned and laughed to Sherpa, "Oh, look at Robert—he's jealous." Admirably on his part, Sherpa gave a look of concern, though if it was for my feelings or because of worry that my often-terrible temper was going to explode was difficult to tell. Then Roza did as no other woman had done before, or since: she grabbed my hand, began lifting me from the snug ("Oh, come on, Robert!") and brought me out onto the dance floor.

I hardly knew what to do with myself. Inebriated or not, I felt as though my face was on fire from blushing. Roza held both my hands as we waited for the band, a quintet of blacks led by a chubby pianist named Kid Memphis, to start up again. Fortu-nately for me, they broke not into one of those flapping, shaking frenzies, but into a slow, tinkling ragtime tune. Roza threw her head back again at the sound, delighting in the maudlin piano, and pulled me close. Her fingers ran along my neck, tugging sometimes lightly at my hair, and I held onto her. Again, it was as though her very fingers were singing, singing this time directly to me, the ragtime rolls spinning up and down my spine. I was transfigured, and transformed, by Roza, by Kid Memphis, by the whiskey and the heat and the money roll and the other couples clutching each other within the Copper Penny, and for the one time in my life I felt as though I had become water. My leg, always so gnarled and gripped and tripping on itself, loosened, becom-

ing water itself, and with it my hips and my hands as well as I pulled Roza closer, even daring to kiss her neck. She did not resist that or my hands now at hers hips tightly, but sighed and shook her hair back so I could kiss even more of her throat as the ragtime piano rolled on and on, and we rolled with it.

After that, all became a wash again. Somehow or another, we returned to the snug, hauled Davidoff to his feet, and were out of the Penny, into the Bowery and back to the Half-Shell, Roza and I arm in arm the whole walk. Barreling through the saloon doors and seeing Maud at the counter, I wondered if Silver was going to be in for it. But Maud said a nary a word, instead disappearing to the back to fetch huge mugs of tea with lemon and a plate of soda bread made just that evening. Chairs were scrounged from various empty berths, and all together we sat, sipping and sobering and smacking our lips at the delicious bread and strawberry preserves. Old Bear came out for the party as well, bonking each of us in turn with his fat black head, and Silver didn't even dispute the cat's Old World origins. Instead, he just yawned and muttered over and over, "What a night, what a night. Not since Pay-or-Play came in at 100-1 has the Bowery seen such a night . . ." I myself couldn't take my eyes off Roza, and my every glance was met with an equal glance. Seeing Davidoff slumped and passed out in his own chair, she rose. I thought for a terrible second that she was going to awaken the schlub so he could escort her back to her aunt's house. Instead, she removed her long overcoat and, with cruel finality, gently covered him with the cashmere. Ever a gentleman, Silver kept his eyes discreetly pinned to his lap as Roza and I ascended the stairs to my berth. Before I shut the door, the top hat was carefully placed on the knob.

The next day, I could hardly contain myself. I escorted Roza—

even lovelier in her dawn disarray—to her aunt's, then fairly raced back to the Half-Shell to boast of my conquest. Enchanted, I had been spared the worst of the binge's aftereffects, but neither Silver nor Sherpa was so fortunate. I found them hunched over in the lobby chairs, moaning, holding their heads, and slurping tea again. Unmerciful, I talked a mile a minute, regaling their aching ears with my exploits.

"You should have seen her! God almighty, but she has the appetite of a man. She asked about the top hat, I made up some dumb excuse, but she brushed my lies aside. 'You're quite the Casanova,' she teased, toying with my shirt as I toyed with the buttons of her cream dress. We were standing near the bed, and then, the dam finally broke. We were on the bed, kissing and kissing and kissing, our clothes getting caught on elbows or ankles, and we began to laugh at our own spectacle. I wondered how she would react to my twisted knee and the grotesque bone, and for a moment I tried to keep it concealed beneath the sheet, but she murmured something I couldn't understand and caressed it all the more, kissing me all over. She climbed atop me, so light and so long-bodied all at once. As I ran my hands over her, I realized with a squawk that she had shaved her pussy! It was almost too much, and she giggled at her own impudence or at my own astonished, excited reaction or both. Then, by god, then we had at it. 'C'mon, Robert, make me disappear,' she teased again as she mounted me, directing my hands and fingers wherever she wished. Gentlemen, we went on for hours, hours, and that is the truth. Can you imagine, a shaved cat! Until you've experienced that . . ."

Too hungover to appreciate the greatness of the night, Silver and Sherpa just gave sickly smiles and rubbed their bloodshot eyes. Then Sherpa asked if the top hat was still on the door, he really wanted to sleep in his own bed; for reasons he couldn't dope out he'd gone to sleep underneath the stage of the carriage house. Such, I suppose, was love in the Bowery.

And such it was. Though Robert, in relating the details of that night yet again to the Harbingers' Club, reveals himself still as somewhat of a braggart, nevertheless, he was undoubtedly in love with Roza. Ellstein and Rouncival were inseparable all during the spring of 1922, taking the new train line to Coney Island, picnicking in Central Park, and generally behaving like lovers in New York City have always done. Though she continued to live with her aunt, Ellstein could be found more and more at the Half-Shell, enjoying time with Robert before and after their mutual performances. Both were gaining fame as crowds flocked to the Bowery to see the amazing young magician and chanteuse hidden at the Silver Stage. As word of their talents spread, so too did their audiences. Scouts for other Yiddish theater troupes congregated at the front benches, while impresarios with open dates at their entertainment halls sought out Rouncival. Along with those having a professional interest in Robert and Roza, others came merely for the spectacle. Among them, in June of that year, was the jazz baby heiress Margaret Tillinghast, and her arrival at the Silver Stage would change everything. No one, not even Ellstein or Sherpa, would have as pronounced an effect on Rouncival's career as the willowy, monied Tillinghast. Some claim she altered Rouncival's path in ways most unbeneficial, while others insist she is due much of the credit for his legend. While we can decide ourselves upon the effect of Tillinghast's entrance in Robert's life, let us, just for a moment, hold the image of Rouncival and Ellstein together, honeymooners surrounded by Sherpa and Silver and Maud and the hapless Davidoff even, a family of sorts formed within, and because of, the Bowery, drinking tea in the lobby of the Half-Shell Palace, a top hat on the doorknob or perhaps a black cat from the Old World brought out for special occasions. As Rouncival himself said, "Ah, but it was a gas to witness."

Well, citizens, we have now seen a case of so-called mass hypnosis. A purely scientific experiment, proving most convincingly that there are no miracles in black magic.

—Mikhail Bulgakov, *The Master and Margarita*

THE
Glass Chateau

Let us stretch. While I hope you have enjoyed your time at the Silver Stage as much as I have, perhaps it is time for something a bit more, ah, active. Come with me to the tall windows, and my, what a day it is! The lilacs, planted by Rouncival as the study was being completed, provide such exquisitely scented shade, don't they? And the marble birdbath you see in the center of the rose garden comes from Ferney, Voltaire's own self-cultivated Eden. Rouncival enjoyed planting rare blossoms and hybrids, though he usually allowed the flowers to be consumed by weeds, witchgrass, and other wild aspects of the lawns and nearby fields. You could say he was a very Darwinian gardener.

Now, before we examine Margaret Tillinghast's influence upon Robert's life, I shall show to you all what the tour brochure has promised: I will reveal the secret of Rouncival's famous illusion of the Glass Chateau. If you would all step this way, yes please, step right up next to the table with that rather yellowed sheaf of papers. The papers are a prescription written by the botanist Carl Linnaeus. Linnaeus, aside from his revolutionary categorizations of plant life, was also a physician who specialized in treating syphilis. Rouncival found this a source of great amusement and purchased the papers at auction for an extraordinary sum. The nearest bidder, the University of Upsala, was highly displeased with Robert's irresponsible spending. If anything, this only made the prescription—a compound of quite innocuous ingredients intended to relieve suffering from boils—that much dearer to Rouncival's heart.

Many of you will have noticed the gun case next to the prescription. Yes, it is a beautifully made case. I shall hold it up so you can all see the inlay. The craftsmen and silversmiths of Seville rarely disappoint. Here too, as I open the case, is Robert's famous revolver. Sadly for the silversmiths, it is a firearm of ordinary appearance though I assure you fully functional. The very plainness of the piece was a key aspect to the Glass Chateau illusion; Rouncival in no way wanted his audiences to believe the gun was special or modified in any way. In fact, he frequently allowed men in the front rows to fire the piece directly at the floorboards of the stage.

Now, I am sure most, if not all, of you have read A. E. Howard's biography of Rouncival. While I might claim hesitancies regarding some of Howard's conclusions, especially concerning Ms. Tillinghast, the work as a whole is a fine one. There is certainly no other that comes within arm's length of detailing Rouncival's illusions during the heyday of his act. While Howard did not consult Rouncival's estate during the writing of the volume, and he was often derogatory regarding the depth of Robert's skills, nevertheless, we do not hold a grudge and at the conclusion of the tour, copies of *Robert Rouncival: Artificer Extraordinaire* will be available for purchase in the foyer.

The one trick not examined in detail by Howard was the Glass Chateau; he makes a few oblique references to it, choosing instead, perhaps because of ignorance, to infer the routine was a minor illusion at best. It was not. Besides being a continuous befuddlement to Robert's audiences, the Glass Chateau also reveals more about the man than perhaps any other of his illusions. Only during his sinister mystery performances would Rouncival dare to reveal so many of his fears, rages, or sorrows.

For you see, the Glass Chateau was a very large, almost bird-cage-like structure, enclosed entirely by tremendous glass panes. Octagonal at its base, with the spire reaching a height of close to twelve feet, the cage was held together by grooved brass rails, which in turn held the glass panes, all of which were the exact same size, in place. A small glass door was the only way in or out of the cage. Rouncival would flourish the gun, allow it to be fired into the floorboards, and then step into the cage. There, he would begin firing wildly in all directions. Above, around, everywhere, bullets would splinter and pockmark the ceiling, the auditorium walls, even a lady's ostrich-plumed hat one time. This would continue for eight, ten, sometimes fifteen to twenty seconds, with the audience ducking, shrieking, and screaming the entire time. Robert paused to let the smoke clear inside the cage, then stepped from the cage to lead a member from the stunned audience up to the stage to inspect the chateau. There, astounded, the shell-shocked assistant would pronounce that not a single pane of glass had been broken, never mind scratched. The combined amazement and relief that no one had been killed would usually result in the audience bellowing with approval as Robert took his bows and Sherpa wheeled the cage off stage.

If you will allow me, we can see a sliver of the effect now, here in the study. Young sir, please step up and inspect the window. Yes, any of them, in fact. Knock on glass, haha. Are you satisfied that in fact this window is as it appears? It is glass, yes? Well, perhaps I wouldn't knock so stridently upon the pane as, yes, it would most certainly shatter and we do not want anyone hurt. Thank you, young sir, you have been a most valuable assistant to me all during the tour. Now, is there someone who is familiar with firearms and munitions even? You, sir, I am sorry to call you out but I see what appears to be a sheriff's badge there on your belt. Haha, yes sir, well, deputy or no, I am glad you could come today with your lovely wife. Would you mind, just for a moment, inspecting the revolver as well as these few bullets? Considering your skill with arms, you may also, if you wish, inspect the chamber of the piece and then load the gun. You are satisfied that this is the genuine article? Sir, I am indebted. Now, if you would all take a pace or two back and keep your eyes on the rather plain looking stone birdbath there in the center of the lawn. No, no, gracious madam, it is not from Ferney, it originates from Dyer's Hardware, just three miles from here. Haha, yes, while perhaps not as audacious as many of this estate's displays, it is nonetheless valuable. Is everyone ready? I would suggest now is an appropriate time to cover your ears. And watch the birdbath!

There! The noise, I admit, is always a shock. It is safe to uncover your ears. I myself shall remove the small plugs, which have caused me a slight grievance from the very beginning of the tour. So, so much better. Now, with the gun back in its case—I shall clean it later—would the young sir mind inspecting the glass again? Right as rain, am I correct? Thank you. That is excellent, as please look out at the birdbath again. It is worse for the wear, correct? You saw the chips flying, Officer? Indeed, they should have, but I commend you on your eye in the heat of fire. Ahhh, thank you, thank you all for such a nice hand. Even in these somewhat diminished circumstances, the effect of the Glass Chateau is a worthy trick, and one I shall now explain.

You see, the large chips and splinters are due to the use of a strangely heavy caliber bullet. While it is certainly capable of causing someone great harm, it is ever so much slower than traditional rounds, especially in these modern times. Nevertheless, to pass through glass? In fact, the bullet did not have to pass through anything until it reached its final appointment with the birdbath. Though hidden inside the walls, the same grooved brass rails used in the Glass Chateau were also incorporated within the study. Catches within the grooved rails release whenever a loud enough noise occurs, and faster almost than the eye can perceive, the glass panes drop only to be replaced an infinitesimal moment later by another pane of exactly the same size. It is a domino effect, and were the panes to be marked, you would now see that every pane in the study has been replaced by another. And within that breath of space between one pane falling and another taking its place, the sluggish bullet passes through. The Glass Chateau, while much more complex, was based on exactly the same mechanism: a loud bang, glass released, a bullet passing through. The illusion is based on timing and timing alone, though it is obviously timing of the most precarious sort. One can only wonder at how many objects were blasted to pieces or otherwise demolished as Robert and Sherpa perfected the routine.

The illusion was actually inspired by one of Rouncival's dreams. In the nightmare, Robert was at the front with his long-dead brother William. There was mud and barbed wire and frozen clotheslines everywhere, and Robert could see William in the distance, alone and wounded in No Man's Land with a

German regiment advancing. Then as Robert began to crawl beneath the clotheslines to rescue William, he was suddenly encased in cold glass, unable to move. He then tried firing his rifle to offer William some cover, and while the bullets passed through, they never hit their mark. Trapped within the glass cage, Robert could only watch as his brother disappeared beneath an avalanche of German soldiers.

Sherpa, who heard the thrashing and midnight cries from the berth across the room, wakened him from his horrors. In a panic, Robert told Sherpa of the dream and it was not long afterwards that Sherpa approached Robert with a strange idea: a glass cage that could be shot at but never hit. Between Sherpa's Caribbean experience with carpentry, hidden holds, and, yes, munitions, and Robert's knowledge of distraction and smoke, they began to work out the details of the Glass Chateau. As an illusion, it was a combined feat and one that does both Robert and Sherpa honor. Nevertheless, it was also an illusion that required much expense to design properly, and it was only through Margaret Tillinghast's funding that they were first able to stage the Glass Chateau in late 1923. If you would permit, one last observation before we meet Ms. Tillinghast. Let us not forget the inspiration for the Glass Chateau. Haunted by a dead brother, a brother whose own predicaments at the front were all too often downplayed or ignored by Robert, Rouncival's greatest illusion was that of himself within an invisible, ever-shifting and unbreakable cage, firing furiously as he hit everything but his mark.

THE
Wampum
Kachina Doll

Please, this way to this rather dark niche of the study. These parts of the shelves seemed to be reserved for some of the more personal effects, though that astrolabe there along the top is reputed to be one of the astronomer Tycho Brahe's instruments. Brahe, a Danish nobleman whose stellar observations would reinforce the concept of a heliocentric universe, lost a significant part of his nose during a duel with a fellow student at Wittenberg. For the rest of his life he wore a metal insert covering the missing aspects. It may be significant that while Brahe's remarkably accurate readings contributed greatly to astronomical understanding, nevertheless, he was unable or unwilling to observe that the earth as well as its sun was in motion. Rouncival had a keen affection for the stargazer and his failings, but unable to unearth the nosepiece he was forced to settle for the astrolabe.

While certainly not as historically relevant as Brahe's astrolabe, you will notice a carved wooden doll on the shelf below. With the bright blue dress, long hair, and the little arms holding what is obviously a small mixing bowl, the doll resembles a Hopi kachina doll. The Hopi, who many believe had their own series of important astronomical calculations, never would have created such a simplistic and obviously second-rate doll, however. This particular piece is Americana of an entirely different sort. During the early part of the century it was included as a small children's gift at the bottom of sacks sold by the Wampum Flour Company. And yes, as I see by your smiles, Wampum Flour with its almost ubiquitous Indian head symbol remains an icon of American industry and home life. Who here has not baked with Wampum Flour? Margaret Tillinghast, sole heiress to the Wampum fortune, certainly did so, for the doll was a toy saved from her earliest childhood.

The Wampum Flour Company was actually established by Tillinghast's grandfather, Frederick Tillinghast. The youngest of six brothers, he sold his share of the family's Baltimore shipping concerns immediately following the Civil War and headed south to make his fortune. A carpetbagger of the usual sort, Frederick took full advantage of the Reconstruction economy and began to purchase flour mills in the ravaged and ravished state of Virginia. He then branched out, using his profits to invest in the ongoing western expansion of the railroads. It was during a visit to one of his rail companies, in the heart of the wild Dakota territories, that the concept of monopolization flourished in his mind. Though not quite on par with Henry Ford or John D. Rockefeller, Tillinghast was nevertheless a forerunner of today's corporate kingpin, seeking domination in certain markets while consistently diversifying his financial interests at the same time. When he died of a heart attack in 1890, his wealth was close to that of Morgan or Carnegie, and Wampum Flour was being sold in its now famous sacks at both coasts.

His oldest, somewhat boorish son, Andrew, and the father of Margaret, managed to finagle a marriage within the upper echelon of Eastern society when he wed the beautiful Lydia Schoharie in 1903. Andrew later gained even more riches through numerous wartime contracts: for a period Wampum Flour was being sold to the U.S., British, and Tsarist armies combined! Andrew's marriage was a disaster, however. The wife Lydia was revealed soon after the nuptials to be a madwoman fond of killing and eating small animals such as rodents or cats. Dead by 1915, the mother spent most of her short, unhappy life within the confines of the Bellevue asylum. The joining of Andrew and Lydia's fortunes did manage to ensure that their only daughter— and there were many rumors that Andrew was not in fact the father—had an entrance to the rarified heights of society. Despite her somewhat Olympian upbringing, like many of her generation Margaret felt disillusioned with the world. She possessed mixed feelings for the source of her wealth as well as what she felt was neglect of her mother at Bellevue, though Lydia's insanity cannot be underplayed: the woman was discovered, wrists slashed, in the kitchen of the family mansion on 5th Avenue frying up a platter of rats. Undoubtedly, she used Wampum Flour to season the poor creatures, and the next morning she was taken away forever. With money to spend and time to indulge her familial horrors and guilts, it is no wonder Margaret Tillinghast took an interest in the sideshow entertainments of life.

It was on just such an excursion that Margaret chanced upon

Robert's act. Under the rakish guidance of her uncle Freddy, Margaret and a number of her similarly wealthy girlfriends decided to seek an evening of illicit enjoyments in the Bowery. Jazz babies all of them, they were bored with champagne parties and the dandified swells at their elbows and desired thrills of a more titillating nature. Uncle Freddy, a dissolute fixture of the horseracing and gambling scene, agreed to lead the women into the bowels of lower New York on Midsummer's Eve, 1922, the night of Robert Rouncival's birthday.

At this point in his life, Rouncival was quite the burgeoning Oberon of his small world. His act was consistently standing-room-only, with more than a few admirers and flatterers in the hotly crowded carriage house. His romance with Roza was equally steamy. According to Rouncival, her portrayal of Leah in Davidoff's flimsy melodrama "The Patriarch" had gone from "a demure yet fearful servant girl to an out-and-out hussy, fairly battering down the tent in order to have at the old man. I believe I had something to do that." We can, as usual, take this with a grain of salt, but nevertheless, with scouts from other Yiddish theater troupes arriving in droves to inspect Ellstein's on-stage presence, she was a woman in full blossom. If surprised that the world was coming to his back alley auditorium, Silver hardly showed it, choosing instead to raise ticket prices on a case-by-case basis: old regulars from the neighborhood were still admitted at a quarter a head while obvious interlopers were charged anywhere from a dollar to two, depending on the cut of their jib.

There is no doubt that Uncle Freddy, with a gaggle of young, wealthy heiresses at his heels, was charged top-dollar after they followed the snaking line down the alley to get a glimpse at the young magician who dared to call himself "Great." I have here letters from a lifelong correspondence between Margaret and her friend Evelyn Blackwood, a niece of the famous founder of Blackwood Movie Studios. While most of the letters from Blackwood were stored in rather ordinary boxes, Tillinghast chose to keep certain notes within the hollow body of the kachina doll. This was done especially in the years after Blackwood's tragic suicide in 1932 when Margaret's half of the correspondence was willed back to her. There shall be more about, and from, Miss Blackwood in a little while, as a future letter of hers contains one of the few actual descriptions of Robert's mystery performances. For the moment, let us think of these women as the debutantes they were at the time, fresh-faced and still relatively unburdened by the sorrows of the world as Margaret writes to "dear Evie" regarding her experiences at the Silver Stage.

Dear, dear Evie,

Oh how sorry I am that you were feeling unwell last weekend; sleep, sleep, then sleep some more if you must, but get better! Nothing is the same without you, and even Uncle Freddy seemed a bit put out when he heard you were unable to join our expedition into the belly of the Bowery. Of course, Freddy is hardly an angel of mercy and you will be relieved to know he quickly recovered his usual good spirits and turned his eye on Janey, who actually seemed flattered by the old goat's attentions. Twice I caught him whispering something closely into her ear, with the dilly giggling wildly at whatever Freddy said. I took her aside a couple of times before the evening was up to warn her, but Janey is Janey and if she has her way she'll end up as a sailor's wife. I know, I am cruel . . .

I shall skip ahead a bit here, there are another two pages of tedious gossip, but first, just a comment on Margaret's sailor remark: considering the future relationship between her and Sherpa, there is an obvious irony to young Margaret's snobbery. Now, where was I? Yes, here. The group has already traveled down to the bottom of the world and is now seated inside the carriage house.

I could hardly believe any of it. Surrounded by Jews and thieves and queer theater folk with long legs and eager eyes, it was almost as if I was young again and being taken to that small, awful room to see Mother. I felt shivers up and down my spine despite the horrible heat within the place. Freddy was still chatting up Janey, by then putting his hands fully on her knees every time he punctuated one of his surely obscene jokes, but I could no longer care. I kept thinking of Mother in the madhouse, Father stopping the hansom on the way home to disappear for quite a while in some gruesome-looking tavern, me alone with my doll looking out the window on the side street, still hearing the screams of the insane as I watched a grubby child steal an apple from a cart and run away. I was so envious that someone could steal, could flee, could fly from the shouting voices into an intimate maze of low-rent neighborhoods and neighbors, to places of soot and sanity and sobriety. Of course, that was a child's dream, there was certainly no more clean living in whatever derelict neighborhood that was than at home, but still, sitting in the audience, I remembered all that as if I had returned again to that place and time, wanting only to steal away again, and then the magician appeared.

As he stepped onto the stage from the shadows, with some kind of strange, turbaned Pundit in robes lurking at his left, the very youth of his face felt like an illusion. I expected an older, almost wizened villain to perform, but there he was, thin and tall and so pale under the lights, blue eyes glistening beneath an unruly mop of sandy blonde hair. Despite still having a shadow of baby fat around his face, he was grinning like the devil himself. He gave a funny, tilted bow, then visibly straightened himself and approached the lip of the stage. There was something not right with the way he walked, but he remained smooth nonetheless, talking all the while to the front rows, some of whom he seemed to know and others of whom he merely teased. A man in a straw boater came in for quite a bit of ribbing before the evening was up. I waited for something to happen, then just as his jokes wore a bit thin, he said, "Would you all hold on for just a moment? I left something back at my hotel," and then he disappeared. Gone. Vanished. We gasped, turning our heads, then a voice from the back of the theater (a grimy, grim place) rose up, and it was the magician, removing a skeleton from a stove in the back. Patting the stove gently, he joked, "It gets kinda hot, but for the price, you can't beat the Bowery. I seem to have gotten my berth for free," and we all laughed, with Uncle Freddy chuckling behind me, "Well turned, young man, well turned."

After that, I could hardly make heads or tails of the act. Despite his youth, the magician cracked wise like an old hand, hardly mentioning magic or illusions or anything, merely performing the occasional wonder as if an afterthought. With the skeleton on one flank and the hawk-faced assistant on the other, he appeared protected from all harms or faults as he whisked back and forth on the stage, every once in a while lapsing into an odd shuffle. Twice he levitated himself, one time appearing in the air with a top hat that rather rudely spilled ladies' undergarments as he said, "Oops," then he somehow made a lit string of candles appear along the brim of the straw boater, ruining that sad piece of apparel. If the man was displeased, however, there was always the assistant there, at times doing little other than in-

timidating the audience with his continuous reptile glare. I found myself fascinated by his silence, and slightly paralyzed whenever his gaze pinned me to the bench. Even Uncle Freddy kept quiet though the magician was walking on air with a revolver in his hands, warning of rats at our ankles. It was one menacing gag after another, with miracles in between, and as the curtain fell, to the skeleton taking a bow in lieu of the magician, I felt a great, great surety: this snake-in-the-grass conjuror could charm or poison any audience he chose to. Even as the people stood and roared, I turned to Freddy, who was equally stunned, and clearly hinted, "With some help, this man could go very, very far." He replied with a look of such viperish appreciation that I actually felt a kind of dismaying pride, "I hope your father is sober enough to write a signature when we return because not even this child sorcerer will be able to make a bank book disappear so quickly. Now, let's corner the bastard backstage before he tries anything else. Let me do the talking, but if that damned Indian fellow goes for my throat, Maggie, you'd better distract him." And with that, dear Evie, we pushed our way through the thieves to befriend the magician.

Befriend young Rouncival they did, and Uncle Freddy must have done his talking very well, for without even any backing at the moment, the Tillinghasts offered to finance a tour of Robert's show, including whatever props, stage devices, costumes, et cetera, were needed in exchange for a fifteen percent share of all future proceeds. Freddy, through his innumerable gambling connections, also knew a fair share of theater impresarios, and he was more than able to impress the young Rouncival with names of managers and places up and down the eastern seaboard. Robert, celebrating his birthday backstage with Roza, Sherpa,

Silver, and a bottle of bathtub gin, could hardly believe his luck. Silver stood up as an agent of sorts for Robert, demanding a contract and asking for but not receiving a promise that the Tillinghast share would come from the net take instead of the gross. Once Robert shook with Uncle Freddy, however, the deal was as good as completed. As the expression goes, "it was all over except for the crying," and the crying would indeed continue for quite some time. By hitching his cart to the Tillinghast fortune, Rouncival would eventually abandon the Bowery, the Silver Stage, the Half-Shell Palace, and Roza Ellstein. While Silver understood the young man's desire for fame in the greater world, Roza was less forgiving. That all should come about on a night when Margaret Tillinghast, in a stupor of midsummer memories regarding her mad, dead mother, should discover almost unknowingly her familial, capitalistic roots only makes that evening that much more remarkable.

Black or otherwise, magic was certainly in the air that night, and along more than one front. Within two years, Uncle Freddy would wed Jane (or "Janey") Beverly, wasting her dowry along with Robert's profits before the stock market even had time to crash. A once promising theological student at Harvard, Frederick Tillinghast, Jr., died of liver disease in 1930. Divorced and living in penury at that point, Uncle passed on to Margaret one of his few unsold possessions, an old Phi Beta Kappa pin. This Margaret kept within the Wampum doll. Now, as you can see, the pin has been placed on the outer robes and the doll appears to have joined that illustrious society. Dissolute baron that he was, Brahe might well have approved of displaying such an insignia of ruined nobility.

A
Recording
OF
"*Solace*"

Before we continue to one of the study's most noteworthy displays, let's pause a moment at the gramophone. Sadly, it is a rather ordinary gramophone: Rouncival near the end of his life cultivated a taste for music, enjoying especially the jazz and blues of such luminaries as Fats Waller, Louis Armstrong, and the gypsy guitarist Django Reinhardt. He also remained true to his dance-hall roots, listening almost continuously to Scott Joplin's melancholic rag "Solace" during his final illness. Yes, madam, I see your nod and agree: as lovely and maudlin a tune as has ever been written, and it is that record which still sits upon the player. For a lion in his winter, surely it must have reminded Robert of days such as this one. Would I . . .? Madam, your suggestion is bold, and appropriate I think as well. Give me a moment to wind the machine, for yes, of course, it still functions, and let us all listen to Mr. Joplin's piece. For those who wish to linger within their own memories, feel free to walk about and gaze at the lilacs while I relate the end of Robert and Roza's relationship.

It was an unhappy ending. Uncle Freddy and Margaret finagled monies from her father, and Freddy booked a tour throughout New England. Beginning September 1922, Robert, Sherpa, and Margaret traveled to Hartford, through Providence and Worcester, then to the once-great Wicklow Auditorium in Boston, and back again to New York City for a standing engagement at the Dappler Theater on Broadway for one sold-out show after another. But from midsummer until the night of his departure, Robert and Roza spent much of their time discussing their future together, such as it was. Ellstein, while wishing to join Robert on tour, felt it was impossible to do so; her professional interests remained rooted in New York. Whatever the source of Roza's sultry allure, her Leah had turned more than a few heads and the Folksbeine Troupe—still performing today, incidentally—was making its interest in her known quite clearly. In fact, they were planning a revival of their already-classic drama, "The Dybbuk," and had offered the female lead to Ellstein, with the show scheduled to start its run in September. Rouncival tried to convince her there would be other parts on other days, but Ellstein knew an opportunity when she saw one. Neither would bend in their aspirations, and thus the relationship was shattered.

They finally had it out in the carriage house, with both claiming abandonment by the other. When Ellstein brought Tillinghast's name directly into the argument, Rouncival would hear none of it, denying any and all attraction to the heiress. At that point, he may have even been telling the truth, but his high-handed manner only infuriated Ellstein all the more. Years later, Rouncival would say of the break, "It was a nightmare. I thought her eyes alone would flay me. I wanted to fall through the trap-door in the stage and make my escape forever. Instead, I fell back on any excuses I could make to try to sway Roza, or at least earn her pity for my situation, but there was to be none of it. In the end, I made a scoundrel's exit, twirling my moustache like a carnival villain as I hissed, 'Then this appears to be the end.' Pathetic! Pathetic! I did not even have the courage of my convictions, but instead left with Roza behind me weeping in pure rage at my idiotic mule-headedness. If I had made even one, small promise to her, it all would have been different. Instead, I relied on my limp and traded the best woman of my life for the filthy whore of Mammon."

Whether Rouncival meant Tillinghast directly by that last remark or was merely referring to his hopes for wealth is unclear. No matter, it was over between Robert and Roza. Coincidentally or not, the very night of Robert and Roza's final argument, the Silver Stage caught fire from a backstage lantern and was ruined as any kind of respectable theater. Crushed by their breakup, Silver himself always claimed that it was the embers of Robert and Roza's fury that engulfed the stage in flames. It would be many years before Robert again trod those charred boards, and then it would be under a different, very infernal guise.

Ah, the music has ended. I did not even notice, I was so absorbed in Robert and Roza. Let me fix the needle, and please, focus on the tall steamer trunk that the gramophone stands upon. The trunk is actually one of Robert's, used early in his career for costumes. During the southern leg of Robert's 1923 tour, when he amazed Savannah, Charleston, Columbia, South Carolina, Raleigh, and Richmond in succession, Robert made a visit to Asheville, North Carolina, to see the final resting spot of Barnabas Welt. While paying his respects, he learned that old Dozy the camel had finally passed on and was buried also at the family's sanitarium. Ordering the costumes dumped or given away, Robert had Dozy's bones exhumed and sealed within the steamer trunk, which he brought back with him to New York. It was the first possession of his actually brought into the study after its completion in 1932. He would often pat the trunk in passing, saying hello to old Dozy.

As for Miss Ellstein, as you all know, she became quite famous with the Folksbeine Troupe, performing at one time or another on six continents. She also has the distinction of being the sole person ever to refuse admittance into the Harbingers' Club. She and Robert had had a reconciliation of sorts, exchanging letters late in his life, but when he nominated her for membership in the club, a nomination seconded by Sherpa, she replied with a very considerate note declining the honor. The letter concluded elegantly, "Looking back on my life, from my aunt's hovel on 6th all the way to the gilded theaters and opera houses of the wide world, I believe I have always belonged to that club. I think, dear Robert, who first met me in a carriage house and lied so sweetly about all the great things you had done, perhaps it could be said it was I who first inducted you into that prestigious company. With Fondness, Roza." Robert was so delighted with the note he had it included in the official minutes of the next meeting.

Roza Ellstein passed away last winter at the age of 103 years old. She is survived by thirty-seven great-grandchildren, with a grand performance hall in Jerusalem named in her honor. Others perhaps did not feel so warmly towards Miss Ellstein: when informed of Roza's refusal to join the Harbingers, Margaret told Robert bluntly, "Thank god! To be honest, that woman always scared the shit out of me."

Houdini's Sleeves

Please, now, just this way a few steps. As you may have noticed, this side of the study contains many objects from later in Rouncival's life. Apparently, he enjoyed having such mementos close to the windows where he could reminisce at leisure, with the mountains across the river as a backdrop. Though today it is a bit hazy about their crowns, the Catskills can be solemn, extraordinary heights in the right light. That Robert displayed his earlier, and often darker in origin, keepsakes across the study within the shadows is perhaps also understandable.

Now, I shall be honest with you and say that I shall not go into any great detail about Robert's most famous period. I am sure many of you are aware of the fortune he amassed from late 1922 well into 1927; otherwise you would not be joining me this fine afternoon. That Robert Rouncival, the second most famous magician of his time, left the limelight at such an early age and retired to this beautiful yet secluded estate in the Hudson Valley hinterlands is not a fact often commented upon in detail. Rather, historians such as Howard chose to focus almost solely on Robert's heyday, and truthfully there is little I can reveal about that time which they have not discussed already. Instead, I'd rather that the tour offer tidbits that are, hopefully, more esoteric and marvelous in nature.

For those who are not that familiar with this period, however, here are a few items key to understanding certain later events. As I said, with Uncle Freddy acting for a time as his booking agent, Robert toured New England, then returned to New York for a standing engagement at the Dappler Theater. The run was a huge success, with the "Wandering Jew" levitation illusion the most well received aspect of Rouncival's act. The Dappler extended the run into 1923, and though Robert wished to begin touring again, with the aforementioned southern leg already being planned, he also realized that the New York profits would allow him to better finance a triumphant swing through Dixieland. It was also during this time in early 1923 that he and Sherpa finally moved out of the Half-Shell Palace. Though the parting was indeed sweet sorrow, as they and Silver had become very close, the old man understood, and it was upon his recommendation that Robert moved all his belongings into an extravagant suite at the now-defunct Peacock Hotel. Located very close to Columbus Circle, the Peacock had always catered to a certain class of individual and wealth, acting almost as a front of the utmost propriety for characters whose monies stemmed from less-than-upright or legal sources. In short, the Peacock Hotel—currently a rent-controlled apartment building with a street-level laundromat and Russian delicatessen—was a haven of feigned decency for scamps and scoundrels, and quite perfect for the likes of Robert and Sherpa. The suite allowed both of them a private bedroom, and never again would a top hat be needed to hang from the doorknob. With the Tillinghast mansion close by on 5th Avenue, Margaret was a frequent visitor to the Peacock, and popular among bellhop and mobster alike for her gauzy charms and breezy laughter.

Following the southern tour, Robert was well established as an act of merit and gate appeal, and managers across the country pleaded with him to perform at their venues. With the Glass Chateau illusion finally ready, Robert obliged them through all of 1923 and 1924, taking only the occasional break to rest and rehearse new tricks within the Peacock suite. From Young's in Atlantic City, to the Crystal Atlanta, to the Orpheum in New Orleans, and then north to the Avenue Theater in Detroit and the Olympic Music Hall in Chicago, Robert and Sherpa and Margaret amazed audiences. Tillinghast had in fact become a minor part of the act, performing her own escape routine from a chained and manacled box. The illusion, an entirely perfunctory bit any child could perform once given the knowledge of the trunk's mechanism, was a hit, however, as Margaret designed her own, rather slinky stage costume. Wearing little but pearls and an opaque, flesh-colored dress, she billed herself as Minnie the Pearl and was allowed once a performance to escape from the trunk, leaping out to the leering applause of the audience and Robert alike. Sherpa too was well aware of Margaret's appeal, looking on like always with the dead vaquero. That Rouncival's act, already admittedly odd, should also include someone other than himself performing an escape was noted, with a columnist for the trade publication *The Daily Magician* writing, "Not that I want to be the only one 'with the grouch' about this, but I really do need to kick about the fact Robert 'The Great' is incapable of escaping from his own magician's trunk. 'Minnie the Pearl' is a looker indeed, and in Rouncival's case she appears to be in 'good hands,' but hang it all, shouldn't a trickster perform his own tricks?" The columnist did go on to comment, "While some of the gags have been performed before Noah, Rouncival's variety, speed, ease, and nerviness will ensure he's well-received again at the Olympia, and anywhere else he displays his wondrous manipulations."

By 1924, Rouncival was ready to take on the Old World, and was booked for a month-long stay at the Cuspidor in London. By this point, Margaret had learned enough from her uncle to begin booking engagements on her own. Besides, the "old goat," as she referred to Freddy, was well into a bender at the time and unreliable for anything. Together, all three crossed the Atlantic in May of 1924, each with their own first-class accommodations. The voyage was a grim inkling of things to come, as Robert took to showing up at Margaret's cabin at ungodly hours seeking company, while she plied him with questions regarding the whereabouts of Sherpa. Though quite the gentleman around Miss Tillinghast, Sherpa remained his own true self by spending much of the voyage with the crew of the liner, either playing cards with the seamen below decks or arranging liaisons with chambermaids in his berth. Though it would be many years before Rouncival was able to laugh about the matter, he did say later, "From the way Sherpa glad-handed the ruffians in the engine room, you'd have thought he was a sailor born and bred, ready to sleep off his grog in a hammock on the deck. But when it came to those chambermaids, well, he certainly had no problems turning in to a first-class berth every evening!" Fending off Robert's advances and intrigued by Sherpa's strange mannerisms, Margaret kept private whatever thoughts she had regarding the former pirate.

That she had such musings in the first place tells much of the story.

The London run was a sensation. Lauded across town, and glad to be in a non-Prohibition country, Rouncival soothed Margaret's continued rejections by imbibing freely and taking full advantage of the many women who sought him out backstage. It was also in London, on the advice of a quack physician/phrenologist, that Rouncival learned of the famous lemon cure for his ailing leg. From London, then to Paris, Brussels, and on to Amsterdam, he could be found after most shows in his dressing area, barely half-robed, greeting the wild women with a lemon, a bottle, and a rapacious grin. That Margaret did not seemingly accept his philandering the way she did Sherpa's was yet another grievance to Rouncival, and as his resentment built he began to refer to Tillinghast's escape trick as "the bitch in the box routine." Rouncival became increasingly moody and hostile to everyone around, and Sherpa and Margaret were often left to their own devices as Rouncival drank and caroused himself to sleep on a nightly basis. Clearly it was time to go home. Sensing the situation was coming to a head, Margaret cancelled several bookings in Germany and ordered Robert, lemon and all, back to the Peacock for some rest. Though petulant regarding lost opportunities for pleasure in the notorious Weimar cabarets, nevertheless, exhausted and with his leg paining him greatly, Robert complied.

The return in late summer was not as docile as Margaret may have hoped. Almost as soon as they had unpacked and settled again in the Peacock suite, Rouncival saw his name in the papers in a most sickening way. None other than Harry Houdini had mentioned him by name, calling his act one "of base instinct, grim shenanigans, and immoral tone. Rouncival is hardly better than the con artists and spiritualist mummers currently plaguing our great country today. So far as his illusions are concerned, he may in fact be decidedly worse." Infuriated, Robert raged throughout the Peacock, limping badly as he cursed the great Houdini with every breath he could muster. Sherpa tried to calm him, and even had Silver come uptown from the Bowery to try to placate Rouncival, but it was of little use. Rouncival's old and trusted advisor managed to keep him confined to the suite, however, saying repeatedly, "Please, Robert, I implore you, this can be discussed, you are a gentleman...." His attempted mollification only fanned the fires, and Rouncival shot off a telegram to Houdini demanding that they meet. Houdini replied rather courteously to Robert's note—Rouncival had actually dared to use the traditional dueling challenge, "I demand satisfaction," in his telegram—and a time was set the next evening. In order to keep the press out of the affair, Rouncival would appear at midnight at Houdini's very lair on 113th Street in Manhattan, the repository of the famous library of arcana, to sort the issue out.

At this time, Houdini was just beginning his crusade against spiritualist charlatans and con-artist mediums. In his efforts to reveal to the public the various methods of duplicity, he also began collecting related manuscripts and letters en masse, and this collection, stored on the second floor of his house on 113th Street, would later be willed to the Library of Congress. It was, and perhaps still is, the most fully realized library of papers on artifice and mystification ever collected. How Houdini came to be interested in Rouncival's act is unknown; perhaps he'd snuck into a show and found Robert's illusions less than sublime. Perhaps he merely felt a moralistic distaste for Robert's gutter slanged patter. Either way, the harsh wording of Houdini's review in the yellow paper the New York *Eagle-Liberty* set the stage for Rouncival's one and only meeting with the confirmed master of magic.

Much of the day of the confrontation was spent keeping Rouncival sober; that Robert would, in the heat of rage, openly insult a prominent figure and then inebriate himself out of having to go through with the actual meeting was a scheme Rouncival had attempted before. The morning of the scheduled duel in the Sheep Meadow, Robert had been so drunk he actually deigned to carry a cane just to hold himself upright. This time Sherpa would have none of it, and despite numerous excuses made to leave the suite, Rouncival was kept cooling his heels until it was time to call a cab. Despite the terrible heat that night, Robert and Sherpa dressed in heavy overcoats and felt hats in order to disguise themselves during the ride uptown. Rouncival couldn't bear the idea of the press getting wind of the moment, and greatly feared he would arrive to a swarm of reporters in front of Houdini's stately brownstone. A thin, greasy rain began to fall during the ride, further dampening Rouncival's spirits, and it was a very grim Robert "The Great" that finally stepped into the steaming street at midnight, Sherpa right behind him.

I have here a short correspondence from Tillinghast, again to Evelyn Blackwood, describing the moment. Though she herself was forcibly denied attending the moment, soon afterwards Margaret received the details from Sherpa with the admonition she keep them absolutely secret. Of course, as such things often go, she then wrote Blackwood as soon as she could, eliciting the whole time confidentiality in the matter. That the meeting did not make the morning papers then or ever is indeed a miracle when one looks back upon it. In the end, perhaps the still-nascent secrecy can be chalked up to the cabalistic ways of the magical and the wealthy alike. It is only our good fortune that Tillinghast and "dear Evie" were such close friends; otherwise that night would have been lost to history. Here, then, from Sherpa through Tillinghast, is the event itself.

One slight note: Margaret at this time did not call Sherpa by that name, using instead the proper "Roberto" when addressing or describing him. That Sherpa often preferred his stage moniker meant little to Margaret until later in their relationship. But enough dilly-dallying.

I had to beg, Evie, beg Roberto to tell me. It took much wheedling and whispery caresses, which as you can guess I quite enjoyed performing and which he seemed to enjoy quite a bit as well. Can the world imagine Minnie the Pearl tickling Sherpa the Silent all over? Let them count the gate on that! I giggle like a fool every time I think of it, which I have to say is very often. Anyway, still, it took some arranging, and I thought it was going to become another Teapot Dome before we finally negotiated a place and time to talk freely. I am sure he felt he was betraying Robert by doing so, but I didn't care. You know how it is—I mean to say, Houdini and Robert, at each other's throats at midnight, and not to know? Impossible!

Our assignation was atop the roof of the Peacock. Robert, the fink, was upstate with Freddy, off to Saratoga and the races. Those horses and hats are only good for a yawn, I think, but I suppose Robert felt losing his shirt on Freddy's awful "insider" tips was a decent way to celebrate the whole incident. Roberto and I met in the lobby. I was sure the night was perfect for our get-together, but then I saw that grotesque hoodlum Lulu Rosen-crantz, pretending to read a paper and staring at everyone that dared pass his huge shoes. I thought, "Oh no, it's off, Dutch

Schultz is staying at the Peacock this evening with his usual gaggle of showgirls, no one move a suspicious inch or we'll all get shot." All was quiet on the front, as the boys say, though, and Roberto led me up a service stairway in the back of the building up to the roof. And you would not believe it but Roberto has created for himself a little cove up there! He has wooden beach chairs, a table, even some tall potted plants, all in the shade where the stairwell opens. It is quite charming, and despite the heat (ghastly, ghastly, I know—when will it end?) the coolest place I have been the entire week. I reclined in one of the beach chairs, he quite charmingly produced a bottle of modestly chilled champagne from a bucket of water, pop it went, and he told me everything, the moon murky and orange above his wonderful little cove.

It seems Robert was quite shaky as he stepped from the cab. The streets were steaming, and mist was everywhere. Neither of them could see very much, and Robert appeared to want to leave, but then they heard a voice above them. Houdini, in evening wear but without a jacket, was out on a balcony waiting for them. Robert, and I have to say he often shows the bravery of a wounded animal, on sighting Houdini screwed his courage tight and called up, "Hah! Is that you or one of your cinematic apparitions?" You know how Robert hates the movies (and who is the lead in the latest swashbuckler Blackwood just released—a god of Olympus hardly describes the man! Go west, young woman, and seduce that Apollo!) and I suppose he meant it as quite the jibe. Houdini just laughed and said he'd be down in a minute.

They waited at the top of the steps and, true to his word, Houdini opened the door himself. His wife Bess was just behind, kind of peering fearfully at the men on her front stoop. They say Houdini is a small man but despite his age still so, so strong, and he ushered both of them inside, laughing at the overcoats as he took them. Robert said nothing for a moment, then pulled himself together and declared haughtily, "Well, Weiss, I am here. Do your worst."

It was a terrible moment. Robert, the bastard, used Houdini's real name as if it was some sort of insult. The pluck! He never, ever gives in. I guess Bess paled at his tone, and Roberto fingered that knife he always carries. I think he must sleep with it. Violence was in the air, air more stifling than breathable. Houdini gave Robert a glare and then stretched one arm out. Blows were about to commence.

Then, rather than send Robert flying as he easily could have, Houdini took a grip of the end of his sleeve and used that famous strength to tear it off all the way from the shoulder! The entire sleeve came away in one piece with that brute pull, revealing his bare arm. Then, with the other, obviously weaker arm, he repeated the feat! Then he opened his arms, nothing up a sleeve because the sleeves themselves were disappeared, and waited for Robert to return the embrace.

Rouncival stared at him for a moment, and poor Roberto was sure he'd do something awful. He was even surer when Robert asked for the knife. Without ever taking his eyes off Houdini, Robert took the knife, flourished it once in front of Houdini's own suspicious gaze, and then, with the smallest of smiles, cut off his own left sleeve at the shoulder. He handed the black silk sleeve (he dresses like an undertaker on Christmas Day, I swear) to Roberto, then hacked off the other. It wasn't nearly as impressive a display as Houdini's, but it did the trick. Both magicians stood, unarmed and grinning, then embraced tightly. The truce stood as Houdini, with many apologies to Roberto, invited Rouncival *alone up to view his fabulous library of liars, sorcerers, and charlatans. Arm in bare arm they ascended the staircase, and Roberto was left to chat and drink iced tea with mint with the good wife Bess, who he said was very charming. It was four hours before the two magicians finally emerged, Robert shaking his head and saying as they came down the stairs, "You know, Weiss, we shall never agree on that point. But at least I understand the road you are coming from." There were hugs and handshakes, the various sleeves were exchanged with many a laugh, then Houdini himself called another cab to take them both home. They arrived at the Peacock in the first red swirls of daybreak, Robert content, clutching Houdini's sleeves tightly and chuckling every now and then. And that was that!*

You will see spotlighted on the wall two rather spacious white sleeves framed under glass. Ladies and gentlemen, I present to you Houdini's sleeves, the sole relic of the one and only meeting ever between Houdini and Robert "The Great" Rouncival. Directly beneath that, also in a glass frame, is the opening, handwritten page of *The Debacle* by Emile Zola. The novel detailed the pathetic collapse of the French people under the Prussian onslaught of 1870. Rouncival could often be found standing in front of these two artifacts, shaking his head and muttering delphically, "The damned thing, the *goddamned* thing of it, is that he was *right!*" Whether he was referring to that secret dispute in Houdini's library of arcana or to Zola's conjectures on courage and cowardice can hardly be known.

THE
Peacock Suite

Ah, what has begun as a fine morning is turning into a fine afternoon. I do go on. Perhaps now is time for an aperitif? I know, it is perhaps not the usual thing to do on a tour, but I believe a sense of intimacy can only enhance the tour's effect. Let us escape the windows—the western exposure is lovely for a view of the mountains but at this time of day, a bit blinding—and make our way to a cooler part of the study.

Please, please, feel free to sit anywhere. There is sangria in the green pitcher and for those wishing maybe something stronger, there is a bucket of ice, limes, and rum in the blue decanter. If you look closely at the decanter, you'll see the inscription is a quote from Frederick the Great: "I begin by taking." The quote was a constant source of amusement for Rouncival as he more than helped himself from the bottle. The rum itself comes from Barbados, where it is made in very limited quantities and is a superior spirit, if I do say so myself. For the young sir or others, there are also colas and iced tea.

Now, the leather couches, chairs, and the settee you are seated upon all come from Rouncival's suite at the Peacock Hotel. He purchased the suite in its entirety soon after the study was completed. There is, however, one chair that obviously does not fit the suite's design. Madam, if you would do me the honor, please come this way and allow yourself to relax here in the wooden beach chair. It is far more luxurious than it would appear. And yes, of course, this is the one piece of furniture remaining from Sherpa's cove atop the Peacock's roof. It was one of Margaret and his most treasured possessions. Haha, yes madam, it is quite the day at the beach, and I am so glad you find the sangria a treat: it is mixed from one of Sherpa's old recipes. Now, as we enjoy the coming of the evening, I shall relate to you the fruition of the romance between Sherpa and Margaret, for how could there be any doubt, and the subsequent catastrophic fallout with Rouncival.

For the three of them, the period from 1924 into 1927 was one of gains, consolidation, and fame. Again, for further details on tour dates and places, illusions, et al., Howard's biography is your best source. What Howard doesn't discuss is that Robert's wealth, now so taken for granted, came in large part not so much from the proceeds of his shows but through sound investment. Often on Tillinghast's advice, he did not sink his funds into the riskier, more fly-by-night aspects of that surging market. Rather, Robert invested in the swelling mechanical necessities of American life such as automotives, oil, and electricity. There is little doubt that without Margaret's hard nose in financial matters Rouncival would have been ruined like so many others in the

Crash of '29. As it was, he survived Black Tuesday handily and in fact spent much of the Depression purchasing many of the fine items surrounding you.

Alongside his wealth, his skills on the stage also deepened. His use of ventriloquism became a staple of the act, with the dead vaquero often adding to Rouncival's patter. More rudely, he would also throw his voice in order to make it appear that Minnie the Pearl's appendages, namely her bosoms, spoke also. This infuriated Margaret, for she had expressly forbidden him to do such, not so much because of prudishness but because Rouncival was invariably very "blue" in his humor when he did so. Though I will not share any of the jokes with you, Robert's puns bordered on the obscene, to say the least.

That Rouncival would continue to mercilessly aggravate Margaret during this period reveals the extent of his own frustration regarding his lack of success in wooing Tillinghast. Throughout all of 1925 and '26, he remained adamant in his belief that she would eventually come to her senses and fall into his waiting arms. That he mingled such gallant gestures as taking her on a hot air balloon ride alongside the New Jersey palisades with much grosser behavior such as the voice-throwing was indicative of the depth of his feelings, and lack of rationale in the matter as well. Robert was certainly tormented by his desire for Tillinghast, a torment only sharpened by their close quarters and constant travels together, but to all but Robert it was obvious that Sherpa and she had the eye for each other. Silver, a steady if infrequent guest at the Peacock, tried to turn Robert's attention elsewhere, even daring to mention an upcoming premiere starring Roza, but Robert was fixated upon the heiress. This fixation was assuaged briefly, then utterly shattered, following a raucous performance in San Francisco in early 1927.

There are truly few details of what happened that night. Rouncival was ending a two-month tour of the west coast, with the grand finale being a weeklong engagement at the Miner's Royale in the Mission District. The act was a hit, the crowds ravenous, and Robert's patter never wittier or more amusing. Apparently, Minnie the Pearl also allowed him far more license than normal, with her bosoms quite stealing the show. That may have been a mistake on her part. In the wild aftermath of the show, when all had gone back to their hotel to blow off steam with a number of hangers-on in what would become an orgy of drink and dance, Robert at some point or another cornered Margaret. We do not know what occurred that evening but it can be fairly guessed that at long last Margaret did give in to Robert's entreaties. In a letter to Blackwood, Tillinghast would say only, "San Francisco began as a dream and became a nightmare. I think I threw my judgment into the Bay that last night. A disaster I wish to forget, though others (No no no, I don't want to talk about it, not even to you, Evie, not now, maybe not ever) prefer to ponder it constantly."

What *is* known is that Tillinghast left Rouncival's entourage the following morning and returned home to New York alone on a separate train. The party wasn't even scheduled to leave the coast for another couple of days, as Rouncival still needed to clear accounts with the Royale's manager, and Robert was left fuming and desperate to know what had gone wrong. When he did in fact return to the Peacock with Sherpa—and who knows what *he* felt regarding the matter—Margaret refused to see him alone under any circumstances, generally avoiding Rouncival and the hotel as much as possible. Claiming that her ailing father needed help managing the family business, she barely budged from the mansion on 5th Avenue. When Robert came to call, she immediately brought him to her father's study, then abandoned him there alone for three hours with the wheezing old boor. Yes, madam, a dirty trick indeed, and returned by Rouncival in spades. His own tactics changed dramatically as he then sought to punish Tillinghast with silence punctuated by scorn. Insulting her wealthy upbringing at every turn, remarking to co-acquaintances on her loose morals, even stooping to insinuate that the apple hadn't fallen far from a madwoman's tree, Robert's attempts at revenge knew no boundaries. Though typically expressing little, Sherpa was infuriated by his friend's behavior and took to occasionally dropping in at the mansion to check up on her, and yes, in his own way, to court her. Considering Robert's splenetic behavior, Sherpa dared not make his move, but it can be guessed the thought was certainly in his mind as Robert's fury inadvertently drove Margaret and Sherpa closer.

It was a spring of discontent at every quarter, and with a summer tour of the Catskill and Pocono resorts scheduled to begin in late June, Tillinghast knew that unless a peace was brokered there was no way they could survive on stage together.

It was again Midsummer's Eve and Robert's birthday when she went to the Peacock Hotel to attempt to repair the relationship. Robert, however, was ensconced in the suite, drinking and brooding heavily on his sour, broken heart. He was incoherent by the time she arrived, mumbling nonsense as he made empty bottles, the bedroom sheets, and even his pistol speak. Sherpa, fearing far worse was to come, quickly ushered her out of the suite and up to the rooftop.

We are again indebted to the Wampum kachina doll, for here is Margaret's account to Evie of that night on the rooftop. Perhaps, madam, you would care to be our reader? To hear a woman of a certain age and experience read the letter of a young lady discovering true love I think would be an exquisite touch. I assure you, the handwriting does indeed betray a wealthy upbringing, as the finely formed cursive is still legible-unto-luxurious after all these years. No? Yes? Ah-ha, see, madam, your fellow tour members stomp the planks demanding your entrance upon our little stage. Bravo! Bravo again, and you shall be rewarded afterwards with one of *the* great secrets of the study: Sherpa's recipe for sangria. Now, if the sheriff would so good as to pass me the decanter, I think I shall, haha, begin by taking some myself. Thank you most kindly, officer. Madam, we are in your hands entirely.

"Ahem. Okay. Um, is everyone ready? Remember, I've had a bit to drink. Yes, well, here goes nothing . . ."

It was ghastly, Robert slurring and lurching all over the apartment, making tables talk and vanishing glasses and having them reappear right beneath his own feet as he stomped on them and shouted "mazel tov!" I felt like I was in the lair of a madman. I don't even know how Roberto got me out of the suite, I was so paralyzed. By the time we'd reached the roof it all broke, and instead of paralysis I felt pure rage towards Robert and his sore head and sore treatment of me, and towards his sore, sordid lies all during the last few months. I wanted to go back downstairs and murder the man or myself, I swear, but I was crying so hard I could barely see. I might have fallen from the ledge if Roberto hadn't pulled me back, sat me in the chair, and poured a hefty slug of rum into a glass (and I do believe the Peacock has gotten for itself a law of immunity from Prohibition; the men in this place are rarely, if ever, without a bottle or a flask right at hand, and thank God for that!).

Feeling a bit better as I drank off the glass and held it out for more, I began to relax and was able to truly cuss that bastard Rouncival out with a proper vehemence. It was almost as if I had gone into delicious shell shock, both limp and extraordinarily clear-minded. Feeling quite good, in fact, I toyed with the palm leaves (where Roberto stole those plants from I'll never guess), enjoyed the sun, and cursed Rouncival continuously for I don't know how long, Roberto laughing softly all the while at his friend's dastardly behavior. I sounded quite the little sailor, making it plain I wasn't going to put up with one more iota of abuse from that . . .

"I'm sorry, but this word, it's . . ."

Madam, I regret to tell you that phrase contains an expletive of the worst sort. Tillinghast was indeed feeling the sailor, and in order to relieve your discomfiture, I shall say the phrase myself; Tillinghast at that point refers to Robert as a "crippled little motherfucker." Madam, you may continue without fear, as the rest of Margaret's account is relatively puritanical despite the actual events.

"Okay . . ."

Finally, steam blown off, I began to enjoy the evening and actually made a few jokes about the lemons Roberto was cutting up for our drinks, saying I hoped the old fakir downstairs would miss them dearly. Roberto lay soaking up the last of the sun (whether because of the act or because we simply enjoy late hours, we are all such creatures of the night—it is rare for any of us to bask in the sun, never mind actually waking before noon) and really, I could only stare as he removed his shirt and stretched out upon a blanket, wearing as always that ridiculous straw hat to keep the light out of his eyes. Seeing all the nicks and scars across his chest and arms, with one very large one stretching practically from his ribs to his hip, I remembered with the usual shock that Roberto had been some sort of buccaneer back in his day. He so rarely speaks of it, and to picture him raiding the Spanish Main, snarling with a cutlass in hand, makes me smile. He is so gentle most of the time, though obviously we both know he is hardly afraid of the ladies. But then, seeing those scars of his made me want to reveal my own, I suppose. Hardly before I knew it, I unleashed my own stays so to speak, unbuttoned my dress (that pretty little blue thing we picked out together last week!) and lay down beside the pirate to sun myself. I think poor Roberto was too stunned to stop me or look away as I've noticed he tends to do when I act bad. But as you know, when behaving poorly us girls can only hope the men will enjoy the view enough to forget their outdated manners and strange shyness. They claim to desire the brazen, but when push comes to shove . . .

Anyway, feeling quite good with myself, and yes, getting a little more than drunk, I lay next to Roberto, occasionally sipping from the glass on his chest. It was truly as if we were stranded upon an isle of our own, the evening settling down, the palm leaves fluttering nearby with the slight breeze, the cars and horns and carters shouting below the roof like waves on an ocean of urbanity. The sensation of being alone, not on stage, not known by any others, was such a relief that I became a bit maudlin, tracing Roberto's scars as I talked about my mother and all those old horrors. Evie, you know that isn't something I have ever felt should be confided to any of my past beaus (well, there was your cousin in Maine that one summer, but you know how that turned out—an ordeal and, I know, one you tried to warn me of beforehand) but Roberto treated the whole matter with such apparent yet kindly nonchalance that the flood gates opened completely. I think he is a man who has seen far more of the world than many suppose, and more than he himself wishes to acknowledge. He took my tears and mumbles in stride the entire time, hardly asking a question, just occasionally offering me a puff from the cigarettes he was smoking and, yes, running his hands all the while across my stomach and elsewhere.

I think Puck must have been about, it was Midsummer's Eve after all, and becoming bored with my own teary life story, I tossed off the last of the rum, rolled atop Roberto and snatched the hat from his head and put it on my own. He most obviously enjoyed our change in posture (a tent pole, Evie, a tent pole) and I played the pirate, growling and giggling such nonsense as "A-vast, ye mateys" and every other kind of hackneyed pirate expression I could think of. Then, god help me, Evie, I took the lemon, squeezed the last of it across his chest and asked that poor man where it hurt.

The rest of the night was spent making love, dozing, telling each other all the times and ways we've thought of each other, making love again, and of course it was all so perfect. At one point I laughed aloud at the scene, thinking of Titania and Oberon, wondering if somehow Robert had become Bottom and I was actually making love to him in disguise. When Roberto asked what I was laughing at, of course I kept that musing to myself. Who knows what illusions we strive under or how or where we are blinded by them, either by ourselves or by the King and Queen of the Faeries amok on Midsummer's Night? As you can tell, my time as Minnie the Pearl in the hands of a magician I have come to despise but sometimes still love (in a fraternal way) while it is his assistant and best friend, the almost silent one, to whom I believe my heart has gone out to, has changed me for better or for worse. I am rambling, I know, but after one escapes from enough manacles and darkened prison-like boxes, it does change one's perspective.

These were just some of the things I thought about the next morning, up so early stretching and sore from the gravel beneath the blanket. I strolled about the rooftop in the hazy light, peeking down at the kitchen boys by the Peacock's back door as they unloaded supplies for the day. I thought of the peacock's tail, of the eyes, and how glad I was at that moment to be out of their sight. Then I thought of how that was only temporary, that I longed as always to make my escape every night, under all the eyes, to every night come upon stage and escape from the chains under the watchful gaze of my newfound lover. With a silent prayer of thanks to good Queen Titania and a pearl earring tossed off the ledge as a sacrifice for those dear old gods we so often forget about, I went to wake Roberto. He yawned and stretched and grimaced from the gravel as well, pulling me close again. As I touched his chest, I saw that a few of the hairs had gone gray (I do not know at all what his true age is) but in the first light, the red dawn had made those hairs seem aflame, as though his heart was burning and burning and burning. It was so much, too much, for me, and I wanted to cry again in pure happiness. I hardly know what happened then, as he saw my tears and picked a lemon peel up from the gravel. Then, with such utter solemnity I thought he was going to announce his suicide, he wrapped the peel around my finger and asked me to marry him. He said he had loved me from the first moment he saw me. He said he thought if we were as one all our days would be like that one was, breaking and red and beautiful to wake to. Of course I didn't believe him at all about the love at first sight and of course I lied also and told him yes, I had loved him from the first moment, and of course, I accepted his gallant proposal on the spot, knowing all the other dandies who'd thrust diamonds rings at me at one time or another would never hold a candle to the old quiet pirate

*who'd first rescued me from an evil sorcerer and then taken me
body and soul on Midsummer's Eve in a rooftop cove above all the
world. With many a giggle and kiss, we staggered downstairs to
tell Robert the good news.*

Madam, allow me. Here is my handkerchief, please keep it, and
yes, Margaret's account does bring a tear to the eye. I must congratulate you upon your reading of the letter, yours has been perhaps the finest telling out of many that the study has heard. Yes,
yes, bravo from all of us, and thank you again.

Sadly for all, Margaret was far, far too sanguine in her hopes
regarding the "good news." Perhaps blinded by their delirium,
the happy lovers did not truly consider the effect their union
would have upon Rouncival. In fact, her and Sherpa's marriage
announcement to the terribly hungover Robert was met with absolute coldness. Straightening himself as best he could, he told
the wide-eyed couple he assumed they would be decamping
from the Peacock and that he wished them well. He then informed them, to their immense shock, that marriage was a sacred
duty, one that required much time and energy, and they would
obviously have no time to continue in their on-stage roles.
Though he regretted the loss of their assistance, he believed they
would be most happy in their life together. He then asked to be
alone in order that he might dress himself; he had that day to find
another assistant for the summer tour.

Margaret and Sherpa were stunned. Even had they considered Robert's feelings in the matter, their dismissal from the act
was completely unforeseen. It wasn't until they had left the Peacock in search of a breakfast at a nearby café that they realized
fully what had happened. Sherpa could hardly speak or eat,
merely rubbing his eyes and occasionally picking up his cup of

coffee and replacing it again untasted. He had stood, thick, thin, and otherwise, next to Robert for close to eight years. They had conned, connived, run from police, starved, frozen, fought barroom hooligans, and in the end grown wealthy together. They were brothers but the brotherhood was broken. Typically, Margaret only grew angrier as the meal went on, finally disrupting the entire café as she slammed the table and cried aloud, "How dare he? How fucking dare he?" But dare Rouncival did, refusing to discuss the matter at all whenever Sherpa or Margaret attempted to broach it. Instead, he would inquire as callously as possible when exactly Sherpa would have his belongings delivered to the mansion on 5th Avenue. Choosing to ignore his own experience with Roza Ellstein, Rouncival made it clear he believed Sherpa was abandoning him for wealth and high society.

It was a week later, right before the summer tour was supposed to begin, that Sherpa finally brought himself to remove his possessions from the Peacock suite. As he did so, with Margaret beside him and Rouncival out somewhere or another, Margaret said at the very last Sherpa stared for a long time at the paper vaquero. Of all the costumes, rooftop chairs, and other detritus of a life on the road, the dead vaquero was all that he really wanted to bring with him. But unable to bear the thought of Rouncival truly alone and unprotected on stage, Sherpa left the paper skeleton behind and closed the door softly. Neither he nor Minnie the Pearl would ever tread the boards again in their lifetime. In a way, neither again would Rouncival.

Though he would go on to perform for another two years, his illusions were more akin to a summoning of Hell than any other kind of traditional stage craft. Adopting a sinister, almost doppelganger-like persona, the embittered Rouncival began to bill himself as "The Sachem Morpho, Master Mountebank." Perhaps one reason for the virulence of Rouncival's bitterness can be seen in the following letter. Addressed to Tillinghast that spring and then returned by post to Robert unopened, the note on mint-green Peacock stationery was only discovered many years later when it fell from behind a section of shelving here in the study. It was one of the most heartbreaking finds Rouncival's estate would ever come upon.

Maggie,

I dream of you, always. When the Peacock couches creak, when the bellhop whisks the doors open, when I get the paper from the kiosk on the corner, it is you I see, always. And it is always you as Minnie that I see, leaping from the chairs, from the magic trunk, from the suite, in the morning, in the evening, everywhere all the time. In your peach dresses and pearls with that easy laugh, I walk with you, talk to you, make love to you and wake to you, imagining that you've never left but are always with me. At night is when I see you most clearly. I lie so still, hot towels on my leg, and I enshroud myself, my arms like a mummy across my chest as I concentrate on breathing, and hearing your breath beside me. I forget where I am, I lose the pains as I float with you, through my life, and how beautiful it is. With you I can go home again. With you and you alone I can sit with my father again, I can race to my mother's arms again. With you I can walk again, not like now, but like now never happened, or any of it. With you, my brother has returned from the war. With you, all those sad animals in the circus, human and four-legged alike, rise again. With you, somehow, I can love even Roza again. We all rise up, we rise and we shine, Maggie, but it is only with you, Maggie, Minnie, whatever your name is. We go on and on, and all the ones we've loved go on as well, crossing a field, dandelion puffs in the air, there is a stream, cows, my brother, my parents, your mother too, Sherpa and Roza and Barnabus and Jerzy and all of them, and oh how wonderful it all is, all of us together, crossing a summer field on our way to another town, and how they'll applaud, oh the hand we'll get when we arrive, tell them all about it, they'll talk for days and days, what an extravaganza we were. It is only with you that I can make those apparitions real. This one time, the only time ever in my life, I will beg: please, Maggie, please be with me in that field. Broken as I am, don't make me go it alone.

Robert

Discovered during minor renovations to the study decades after Rouncival's death, Robert's plea, minus any claims to greatness, was never heard in his lifetime.

Blue Flames

Sachem's Cave

Onwards! Come, let us stretch and please, this way. And yes, just leave your glasses on the table there, haha, it will not be the first time the Peacock suite has seen a slew of empty drinks.

Yes, yes, right this way along the wall, and there you'll see being used as a bookend a rather largish chunk of masonry. Look closely and you'll see it is an inscribed relic from the Mayan ruins of Chichen Itza. That the ancient Mayan astronomers and mathematicians had calculated the date of the end of the world down to the last minute but never invented the wheel was again a bit of trivia that tickled Rouncival's fancy. In fact, the entire Mayan empire went extinct or disappeared without any obvious cause, a historical oddity Rouncival also felt was significant. Now, archeologists believe that it was either a failure of arable land or continuous internecine warfare that led to the end of the mighty Mayan civilization. Chichen Itza itself was a site of human sacrifices, with many bodies discovered at the bottom of its holy well.

Grim, I know, but perhaps no darker than the next chapter of Robert's life. We can pause right here, and please, if you could, would everyone crowd as close as possible into the niche? A suit of armor was originally going to inhabit this spot, but when Rouncival was unable to procure one of Henry VIII's childhood suits, he left the cornice empty except for the lanterns you see hung on either side of you. As you can tell, even in the sunny expanse of the study, this particular area does not receive any direct light, ever. If you would allow me, now I will light the lanterns. Ah, where are those matches . . . ? Yes, right here. All right.

I agree: the effect is somewhat disturbing. The lanterns, carefully constructed by Robert, have many tiny pinholes in them in order to create fiery patterns when lit, and as you can see, the patterns are of swirling skulls, devils, vapors, and flames. But there is more. There are two small bowls also mounted on the walls, each containing a chemical compound. Though I have already revealed the secret of the Glass Chateau, I will refrain from giving away all the spells of the magi. Know only that these compounds are completely safe and formulas for such can be found in any junior magician's trick book. What are they for, you ask? See here: toss a pinch of this dust into the lantern and voila, the flames change color. Blue for this lantern and I think we shall use green for the other. The effect is, as you can tell, even more melancholic, as though the apparitions flickering on the walls have gone cold. The flames, so to speak, have lost their life.

During his performances as the Sachem Morpho, Rouncival had many, many such lanterns burning on all sides of the auditorium, each swirling with different devils, death-heads, and obtuse hieroglyphics. He also quite illegally added yet another compound to the flames, with small bits of opium embedded within the burning candles. The sweet-smelling narcotic would slowly fill the small theater to the rafters, gently lulling the audience into another, twilit world as Rouncival took full advantage of the hazing of the audience's senses. His most diabolical and far-fetched illusions were always saved for the end of the act, which often went on for an extraordinary three or four hours. That the act, an opiated form of survival contest for the audience and Robert alike, was performed in one venue and one venue only, the burnt-out stage of Silver's carriage house, only made the show that much more of a journey to the netherworld.

But I am getting a bit ahead of myself. It was not until the winter of 1928 that Robert actually took the stage again at the carriage house, or anywhere else, for that matter. His threat to Margaret and Sherpa that he was out to find another assistant was merely a ruse. Rouncival in fact cancelled his summer tour at the last moment, much to the outrage of booking agents and resort managers across the northeast. Any number of suits were filed against Rouncival regarding his cancellations and broken agreements, all of which he put off for as long as possible before settling: he mostly wished to aggravate those who had dared file against him and he took every measure to make the legal process as much of a drawn-out ordeal as possible. Despite his continued gate appeal, Rouncival burned more than one bridge, to say the least, as he spent the entire autumn of 1927 sulking at the Peacock suite, hardly seeing anyone and generally leaving the hotel as little as possible. It was during this time that he became an acquaintance of the bootlegger Dutch Schultz, who, as Margaret noted previously, stayed at the Peacock during downtown business meetings and post-Broadway revelries.

As for Tillinghast and Sherpa, they did in fact move Sherpa's belongings to the house on 5th Avenue. Though her father was somewhat put back by Sherpa's obviously Latino appearance, the old man was too sick or unintelligent to raise much of an issue regarding his daughter's in-house lover. Though he would occasionally fuss and threaten to disinherit Margaret, Andrew's bloated complaints were perfunctory at best: Tillinghast knew he would never actually leave his sole heir dangling. In fact, after Margaret and Sherpa eloped at Niagara Falls, with Evelyn Blackwood serving as the maid of honor and Bill Silver standing up for Sherpa, Andrew Tillinghast actually shook Sherpa's hand and congratulated the couple upon their return. If their union was sordid, at least it had been made sordid in the eyes of God, and that was enough to placate the old man's atypical conscientiousness. For safety's sake, Margaret did not inform him she had changed her name, and was now officially "Margaret Tillinghast Hernandez," though for clarity's sake I shall continue to refer to her as Tillinghast. The marriage did make the scandal sheets, however, upsetting both the Schoharie side of Margaret's family and Rouncival greatly. Shunned by many but uncaring, Sherpa and Margaret were left to their own paradise, honeymooning at the mansion and strolling the autumnal expanses of Central Park, forgetting as much as possible Robert's icy fury and the vagaries of their future together.

It was late February before Rouncival was able to rouse himself from his gloomy lair in order to meet with Silver at the Half-Shell Palace. During his time of self-imposed confinement, Rouncival had conceived of a new kind of act, one he wished to perform only under a given set of conditions, and the partially ruined stage of the carriage house was the ideal setting. It was again a frigid day when Robert limped through the saloon doors to discuss his plans with Silver. Like many in their circle, Silver had benefited greatly from Margaret's financial advice and he was doing quite well for himself. Silver kept the Half-Shell open mostly to keep in touch with the Bowery rascals whose company he enjoyed so much. Despite not needing the income and being thoroughly disgusted with Rouncival as well, Silver agreed to let Robert pay for modest repairs to the carriage house seating, though Rouncival insisted the ashen stage and ceilings remain untouched. He also refused to tell Silver the nature of his act, preferring instead to create as much of a secretive sensation as possible. Rumors of Rouncival's reappearance were carefully leaked to broadsheets and dailies across the city, with a date, time, and location given though never quite promising that Rouncival himself was going to be in attendance. Additionally, special invitations were sent to select VIPs, including Dutch Schultz and Evelyn Blackwood, with the invite to Blackwood obviously meant to irk Tillinghast. Rouncival's use of the title "Sachem" was also a thinly veiled dig at Margaret's Wampum fortune. Columnists noted that the seedy location was in fact the first stage of Rouncival's career, and the city fairly buzzed as opening night approached. All were aware of the momentous fallout, and all wanted to see what illusions the magician would unveil in his first-ever solo performance.

It is a very fortunate thing for us that Robert did invite Blackwood, no matter how cruel his intentions may have been, as her account is the sole complete testimony ever of Rouncival's mystery shows. Though the act did receive several reviews, most of the journalists were either too flabbergasted or flummoxed to describe Robert's illusions in any detail. Blackwood herself had become somewhat of a figure of notoriety. Disdaining familial pleas that she take to the silver screen—with her heart-shaped face and bowtie lips, she was quite the vixen—Evelyn had become a poetess of some note. Though her imagistic verse was not nearly on par with that of William Carlos Williams, she did have several volumes to her name and was considered a rising, if laborious, member of the poetry firmament. Though most of her verse is now forgotten or considered amateur, her volume *The Crater's Gaze*, written in 1931, is still read as a minor precursor to such later voices as Plath and Sexton.

I know several of you may feel a certain amount of claustrophobia standing here amidst the vapors and infernal shapes. If you wish you may take several steps back as I shall read Evelyn's letter to Margaret from the back of the niche. The light, such as it is, is enough to read by. Also, I believe this is an account best heard emerging from darkness.

Maggie, I am sorry but I was unable to resist. If only you had seen Robert's letter: gold-inked, black bordered, with these strange, almost medieval monkeys climbing the letters—it was either an invitation to a funeral or a farce or both. I know, you may very well wish it were a death notice, I am sure I would if our situations were reversed. Still, the spectacle alone . . .

Your description of that wretched little alley with the theater at the very end hardly does the lane justice. I asked Maurice—just arrived in town and a criminal wag at times but fine as a bodyguard—to accompany me to the show. I gripped his elbow tightly as we ventured down the alley, shuffling through the cold with the rest of the crowd, all of us shivering with excitement. There was a great line near the doors in that little square you described so perfectly—yes, it truly feels though you are trapped at the bottom of a well—and standing there I saw a pack of gangsters with a foul-mouthed hood at their center. Of course I recog-

nized him from the papers and despite myself I began to point and say to Maurice, most likely far too loudly, "Holy shit, that's Dutch Schultz..." He quickly pinched me, hissing that I should hush up, and I suppose it was wise advice though I can't say it added any to Maurice's charm. He really does lack imagination, further proof Hollywood requires very little of a leading man. I know, you enjoy swooning over them so—daydreams, Maggie, and not especially nice ones when faced up close.

By the time we reached the door, we could finally see the marquis, such as it was. A crudely painted billboard hung from the eaves read only, "The Sachem Morpho, Master Mountebank, Appearing Tonight—10 PM—Sold Out." There was no mention of Robert at all. Maurice gave a scowl and said something nasty about a waste of time and some party he was missing uptown, and this time it was me that gave the pinch and advised shutting up.

Inside was the most controlled mayhem I have ever seen. It was also creepy to the extreme. You told me there was a fire, but I could not imagine. All was charred, all seemed to drip, as though the firemen had only just left. It felt like a cave, and the steaming, suddenly sweaty throngs only made the fug worse. Not only that, but lanterns were hung everywhere, all burning with a thick, sweet smoke, each casting hellish figures on the walls. And I do mean hellish, Maggie: skulls, devils, wisps of hellfire, each figure rippling a bit whenever someone passed, as though it were their shadow. I thought we had fallen into Hades for a moment, and I jumped like a mouse when Mr. Silver touched my arm. You are so, so right, a dear man, courtly in his way as he said we had places reserved in the front row. He also seemed nervous, though I truly don't believe he had any clue whatsoever what was go-

ing to happen. He escorted us down the center aisle, and I could hear the newspapermen whispering as I passed. The Dutchman wasn't enough, I suppose, to satiate those jackals, they needed movie people as well to top their yellow headlines.

Honestly, as I sat down, that theater was the last place on earth I wanted to be associated with. With the blackened timbers, sweaty walls, drifting smokes, and vague skulls leering from every wall, my skin crawled as though I had just stepped barefoot on a bug. Having that killer Schultz sitting a mere foot away didn't help my nerves any. He was in the front row also, chomping his cigar and squinting nastily at anyone who dared cough or make a noise at all. Now I know what you meant about him at the Peacock: his presence alone gives the impression someone is going to be murdered at any moment. My nerves certainly felt shot, the theater was so oppressive, and my courage almost failed. I was even about to insist that Maurice get me out of there and back uptown to any party at all, it didn't matter just so long as we escaped that terrible place. Then the curtain rose, and it was too late.

Much to my surprise, it was dear old Silver on stage, kind of quaking. He announced that there was to be a short musical preamble supplied by his wife, Maud. The Sachem Morpho—you think cowardly Robert would dare use that name if Sitting Bull was seated in the gallery—I doubt it—in Robert's case it is more like Limping Bull—was still preparing himself, claimed Silver. Then Maud herself came on stage and sat at a piano half-hidden in the shadows downstage. You always told me she was a sickly, thin woman, but jesus, Maggie, with that nose, gray face, and mousy hair, a thinly skinned witch is more like it. She seemed to be as much smoke as whatever incense Robert was burning in those lanterns. *She almost dissolved into the background as she seated herself on the bench, and then, christ almighty, then she played.*

It was an exquisite torment. The program itself could not have been more proper, nocturnes from Chopin, and her playing, even if a bit robotic, was skillfully done as well. But the piano, charred like everything else, was out of tune. Not completely out of tune, but certain notes clanged terribly in the midst of that gorgeous, dreamy music. Silver, near the edge of the stage, paled as his wife played, her head nodding up and down to the slightly slowed pace of the nocturne—C minor, if memories of lessons with Sister Riley serve, and normally such a perfect piece. I felt myself almost mesmerized by the performance, one moment closing my eyes, envisioning the romance of the tune, envisioning a stormy night, castle walls, a window open, a woman's head emerging, searching the stormy wastes for her lover. But then a note would be so off-key I was jarred from the reverie, almost physically pained by having to come to my senses in that grisly place. Somehow, even the hope of the dream woman's longing had been taken away. All that was left was the cold.

Maud completed her recital to silence. Finally, a few began to applaud limply as she stepped off stage without even a bow. Maurice just glared at me, making it clear the evening was off to a disastrous start so far as he was concerned. I was too moved, in a fearful way, to know quite what I felt. Then we waited. One minute, two, three. Nothing. I could hear Schultz growling through the smoke clouds, and then Robert entered.

Oh, Maggie, I am so glad you could not see him. He was gray. Not just the usual pale of wintertime, but genuine pallor. Even his eyes—we both know how blue they can be—seemed dull. He was all in black, of course, but as he came center stage, I noticed that he no longer bothered to conceal his limp. In fact, he almost seemed to accentuate his difficulties, thumping, thumping, thumping on the ashen boards. Then he stopped, drew himself up, and gave the smallest, slightest bow. And the look on his face— scorn, Maggie, that is all one could call it. Scorn for the theater, scorn for us in the audience, scorn for himself as he rubbed his leg and shot his cuffs. I wanted to cringe, to crawl beneath my seat, closing my eyes in the childish hopes that would make me invisible. Even the Dutchman felt it as I heard him murmur, "Christ..."

"Good evening," said Robert. Then he waved his hands at the lanterns nearest the stage and the flames became blue. A dark, cold blue. Then, doused in that cold, iceberg light, he began to tell us about his childhood. Maggie, I swear, that was all, that was the illusion as he described a place he had been somewhere upstate called Burden Lake. It seemed so simple, him telling of circus folk and farmers and village dullards, but as he did so, other voices began to emerge. Terrible voices, cursing voices, choked and angry and embittered, all those farmers and circus folk speaking from the blue lanterns, throttled and almost drowned-sounding. And each told of their burdens, of their poverty, of freezing, coal-less winters, of beasts dead in fields, of crops failed, loves lost, and serpent-toothed children; of the cuckolds and adulteresses, of slavery in the cages of freak shows, of slavery in the center of the circus ring, of slavery to landlords and bank officers and greasepaint. All those voices, each one hopeless, shamed, and raging, drowned within the blue flames of Burden Lake.

Then it was over and I almost gasped to see Robert alone on stage. It had been another world, other people, a realm unseen, but there he was, just Robert in black, suddenly silent. Even Maurice was agape, all of us were, really, as Robert began another tale.

It was hardly even a story; he more posed a question, asking us if we had ever spent midnight in a switching yard. He cast his hands towards the lanterns again, and this time the fires became sizzling red. I could hear him pacing on the stage, thump, thump, thump, and the sound and scrape of his boots began to sound like trains rolling in the distance. The stage felt as though it expanded, becoming one of those morose prairies, and slowly the yells of tramps and hoboes could be heard, along with the occasional steam whistle. The tramps were jumping, jumping from the freight cars as Robert told of a fire one time in the switching yards, of the railroad bulls racing through the empty lots and tracks, of police and fire brigades swarming the yards as hoboes begged and were beaten and arrested, some burnt alive, screaming in the roasting cars, the door handles melted or too hot to open. It was terrible, and I heard myself cry out for a moment, hardly aware anymore of where I was, but I just wanted it to stop, and then it did, Robert alone on stage, one arm thrown around that damn skeleton he always uses. He was smiling as though the trick had gone off even better than he dreamed. He made me sick, and I rose, so angry at him, at such a cheap, vicious trick, but he raised a hand and I sat again, stunned and wondering what next.

Then he said his next trick was inspired by the sporting world. Now we both know he doesn't care a whit for baseball or those college boys mugging each other on the gridiron, but he said he'd seen something in the papers about a lineup of men known as "Murderers' Row." A number of the audience gave slight whoops regarding the Yankees, Schultz included, and we all felt as though "At last! Just a regular old magic trick, now the fun starts." We were wrong, though, as the flames turned green and Robert then promised to tell the fortune of "the unlucky nine, our own little Murderers' Row so to speak." Then, the bastard began to select members of the audience, pretending to forecast their future as he posed questions and let the skeleton answer. And every answer was horrible! Death, loneliness, fear, those were Robert's prognostications! He spoke to me, Maggie, and I can't even repeat what he said, it was too damn awful. For others it was just as bad or worse. After being told her infant son would not survive the polio, one woman collapsed to her knees weeping, her husband outraged and screaming he would kill Rouncival. But Robert only worsened, actually relishing the threats from the audience. He displayed a pistol holstered at his shoulder and pointed at the skeleton with a shrug. Christ, Maggie, it was the act of a snake in the grass, claiming innocence even as it brandished its fangs. Still, the pistol may have been a bad call, as the Dutchman's thugs rose as one, pulling their coats back to show their own guns. The Dutchman was roaring, but still Robert showed no fear. Instead, he bellowed, so strange to hear from such a slight man, "Now, now, Mr. Schultz, would you hear your fortune?"

Schultz was standing, glaring at Robert. Then he spat, "Yeah, chief, go ahead. Tell me my future," and everyone knew that it didn't matter what the skeleton said, either way Robert was already a dead man as far as the Dutchman was concerned. Robert then held his head as though channeling the spirits, and the skeleton said, "Talk to the Sword." The Dutchman just blinked, we all did, it was just so strange, and the skeleton repeated, "Talk to the Sword."

"What the fuck . . ." whispered Schultz, and now he seemed scared, as though a hidden nightmare had come alive in front of his eyes. The green vapors on the walls seemed to ebb and flow, breathing, and this time it was the lanterns that spoke, hissing like wraiths, "Open this up, break it so I can touch you." It was as though the flames were trying to lick Schultz's very soul. He just

took a step back and shook his head, trying to clear his mind. The haze throughout the room was so sweet, too sweet, then the skeleton caterwauled, "Oh, I forgot I am a plaintiff and not defendant." The green flames raged, the devils dancing and shrieking, singing the melody of Maud's off-kilter nocturne until the devils, the fires, the skeleton, and the walls themselves rose in one final gust, chanting again and again as they faded, "The Baron does these things, the Baron does these things . . ."

Then it was over. The lanterns returned to normal, the walls ceased to spin, and all of us, the Dutchman as well, found ourselves standing, swaying dizzily as Robert thanked us. All he said was, "I am the Sachem Morpho. Good evening." Silver was too confused or horrified to remember to drop the curtain but it didn't matter, Robert was gone, into the shadows. The only one unfazed was Maud Silver, who just clapped her hands a couple of times and then walked out, probably back to that damned black cat you told me about.

I don't know how Maurice or I finally escaped the theater. All I knew was we were outside in the courtyard, breathing the cold air desperately, trying to regain our senses. I could see tears in his eyes, who knows what nightmare he had been living throughout that perverse performance. We were, all of us, in different states of shock. Scared, angry, sorrowful, it didn't matter; we were like ghosts of ourselves, stripped of our earthly lives by Robert's lies, thrown voices, and death sentences. Maurice showed me his watch: we'd been under Robert's spell for three hours!

As we reached the end of the alley, I could see the Dutchman trying to relight his cigar. A car was pulling up, and his cronies were keeping a close eye. As we passed, I heard Schultz mutter to one of his thugs, "That man ain't no goddamn magician, that's the *fucking devil. Lulu, tell Billy to check us out of the Peacock, no fucking way I'm going back there, not with him around. Now get me back to the Bronx before the goddamn cold kills me."*

Please. Let us step out of the lantern niche. Yes, we could all do with the light from the windows. See—a lovely summer evening. Just a few brief remarks before we continue. Rouncival's performances as the Sachem Morpho were quite probably his finest illusions ever. That we still have little idea how he managed to affect his audiences to such a degree is further testimony to his abilities. As for Evelyn Blackwood, despite the critical notices accompanying *The Crater's Gaze* in 1931, soon afterwards she was a woman drowning in despair. She fell in love with the aforementioned Maurice, though he himself was homosexual, a fact the movie studio suppressed with draconian measures. I am sure you can now guess who Maurice actually was: Maurice "Mo" Standish and a legend of the early cinema if ever one existed. He too was tormented, genuinely caring for Blackwood and feeling an immense guilt regarding her obsessive love for him, but the situation was impossible. Evelyn Blackwood committed suicide in 1932, ingesting a bottle of vodka and an entire bottle of sleeping pills before she walked into the ocean near Big Sur, California. Standish lived on, wealthy and famous and very unhappy, until his death in a car crash in 1947.

As for Dutch Schultz, his story is also very famous. In 1935, on the lam from law and criminal alike, he was ambushed and shot repeatedly at his hideout in New Jersey. Lingering for any number of hours in his hospital bed, Schultz gibbered incoherently as a police stenographer recorded every word. More than one of Robert's prophecies would be heard again as the Dutchman lay dying. Of course, whether such is proof of Robert's ability to read a person's soul or is mere coincidence is a question of personal belief. Either way, Schultz's ravings didn't contain any clues pertaining to his killers. No one was ever found guilty, or even identified, regarding the crime.

Vanya's Program

This way, to the desk near the back of the study. Yes, young sir, I would second that sigh if I could: it is a relief to be away from the blue cave. Of course, I am assuming the exhalation was not one of boredom.

Rouncival purchased this desk and the accompanying chair at a very dear price in 1933. The stately yet simple design of these pieces belies their origin from the White House. No, haha, not the White House that usually comes to mind first, but rather Anton Chekhov's summer home in Yalta, a rambling structure known to locals as the White House. Even among the ostentatious mansions of that Crimean resort, Chekhov's home was nevertheless very distinctive. Many of the famous writer's frequent houseguests found the asymmetrical, light-filled home the epitome of comfort and relaxation. Built without any architectural style in the corner of an orchard, the White House was the residence in which Chekhov wrote perhaps his greatest short story,

"The Lady with the Pet Dog." Rouncival was able to secure possession of the desk and chair only through very complicated maneuvers involving a corrupt Soviet official who stayed for a time in New York City. Stalin, not coincidentally, recalled the official immediately after the desk set was discovered missing.

You will notice also, in the rather delicate frame, a typical Playbill theater program. While the front cover is sadly missing, the program is in fact from a showing of Chekhov's masterpiece *Uncle Vanya* at the Cort Theatre in 1930. The excellent cast, with Kate Mayhew and Osgood Perkins and directed by Jed Harris, also included a star of the silent screen: Lillian Gish. After an absence of seventeen years, Miss Gish had finally returned to the stage.

What is ironical regarding her triumphant return to Broadway is that it precipitated Robert's forsaking of the limelight. Robert's dislike of the cinema is well known, though he did slightly prefer the silent films to the burgeoning "talkies." He was also a showman who kept an active eye on any theater activities, and he made sure to be present for the opening night of Miss Gish's sensationalistic return at the Cort. The theater more than matched Gish's star appeal: built in 1913, the Cort was modeled on the Petit Trianon in the royal city of Versailles. With its dramatic detailing and elegant interior, the Cort further echoed its palatial origins with a mural depicting a dance in the gardens of Versailles.

Aside from being able to gaze directly on the lovely Miss Gish, Rouncival by 1930 must certainly have enjoyed spending, and even needed to spend, an evening in the luxury of the Cort. His life, for all intents and purposes, had become a nightmare, and one he replayed on stage four nights a week at the carriage house. His continued performances as the sinister Sachem Morpho had taken their toll. Aside from his still heavy drinking and no-doubt indulgence as well of the opium he so effectively incorporated into the act, Robert's leg also was worsening by the day. If he exaggerated his limp at the beginning of his tenure as the Sachem, within a few months exaggeration was no longer necessary. The three-to-four-hour shows were slowly but surely wearing his joints down. Arthritis, blood clots, even strained tendons, were becoming routine for Rouncival, who continued to perform through the terrible pains. This of course only damaged the leg further, which then drove him to imbibe more in order to dull the pains, which in turn contributed to the misanthropic darkness of the act. Rouncival added by late 1928 a "Suicide Hall" routine that equaled the unpleasantness of his other Morpho illusions. From the brief, rather discombobulated reviews we have of those shows, "Suicide Hall" was as if the worst of the Bowery had come to life, howling their pains and addictions, pounding on the rafters of the carriage house like so many demented poltergeists.

Rouncival's vicious, downward spiral was only enhanced by the company he kept at the Peacock, as he took for a lover one Miss Hilary Graf, a minor figure of the Prussian nobility in exile. Ruined by the Weimar recessions in her homeland, Miss Graf came to America, lived courtesy of the goodwill of other monied exiles, then became a devotee of Rouncival's mystery shows, appearing front and center for each and every performance. The Sachem Morpho reminded her of amoral, sadistic cabaret shows of her homeland, and Robert couldn't help but notice his newest, greatest fan. During her time with Rouncival, they mostly lurked about the apartments in the Peacock, drinking, smoking, and furthering each other's depressed alienation. It was a match made in Hell, and later Robert would snarl of Graf, "A vampire too stupid to realize how little blood I had left to give. Wherever she is, I hope she's dead with her head cut off." Robert's seemingly cruel comments hardly stretched the facts, and truthfully, the less said about Miss Graf the better. A callous, embittered woman, and one who in many ways typified the Sachem's fans, she would return to Germany fully in thrall to Hitler's fascist, racist rise. She went on to marry an officer in the Gestapo, and both were killed during the Allied fire bombing of Hamburg. Whether Robert's wish for decapitation came true is unknown.

Though far nicer, this period was one of isolationism for Margaret and Sherpa as well. Andrew Tillinghast's health was declining badly, and more and more it was up to Margaret to keep the family concerns intact. Among those concerns was her stake in Rouncival's gate proceeds. Well aware of the Morpho shows, she sued Rouncival in order to claim her fifteen percent cut. Rouncival, of course, refused to hand over a single dollar, and attorneys for both had to settle the matter. Neither Margaret nor Robert would attend any meetings, and it was the lawyers alone who sealed Robert's buyout of the Tillinghast share. All in all, Margaret was equal to the financial challenge, and despite a few unavoidable setbacks following Black Tuesday, her fortune remained generally healthy as it headed into the Depression. The same could not be said for Andrew, whose heart finally gave out in very late 1929. Hoping to cheer a few family and friends after the crash, Margaret threw a small holiday party at the mansion, but the combination of company and flaming rum raisins did Mr. Tillinghast in. He collapsed in the kitchen and one of the servants, believing he was merely hyperventilating, held a Wampum Flour sack over his mouth. Margaret found her father dead on the floor, covered in flour, with the sobbing servant and crushed sack next to his head. Grieved and believing she too was cursed to die a grotesque Wampum death, Margaret rang in the New Year a sadder, wiser, and even wealthier woman.

As for Sherpa, he was finding that the life of privilege and endless ease was becoming a bore. Though he certainly assisted his wife in keeping the family empire strong, he was not, how shall we say, fit for placement on the board of directors of a railroad. As you can imagine, such duties could only have led to disaster. Several, more appropriate maritime options were discussed, as Margaret still had some connection with the Baltimore shipping business, but in the end neither she nor Sherpa were willing to relocate to that notoriously dour city on the Chesapeake. For a time, they even considered trying to make it a go of show business again. Despite advising against any dealings with Hollywood, Evelyn Blackwood did offer to introduce the two of them to her mogul uncles in charge of Blackwood Studios. The three traveled to the west coast in early 1930 to scout the possibilities, but while the vacation provided Margaret with a much-needed bit of sunshine and escapism, overall both she and Sherpa found the delights and deceptions of the movie world lacking. Stage sets and cinematography paled in comparison to the very real illusions of unbreakable glass, bullets, and slipped manacles. Typical of Margaret, though, she recognized a goose with a golden egg when she saw one and invested quite profitably in Blackwood Studios immediately after the visit. Tragically for all, Evelyn stayed in Los Angeles on some family matter or another, and thus began her catastrophic affair with Mo Standish.

All in all, the couple returned to New York at loose ends. While Margaret had finances to take care of, Sherpa especially longed for something else. Remembering the tools and belt Thomas Rouncival had given him so long ago, he rented a small storefront just off Columbus Circle and opened a watch repair shop. Business was, of course, almost nonexistent, but it hardly mattered. Sherpa had a place to go every day, and as spring flourished he took to sitting on the sidewalk in front of the shop, with a table and potted palm tree nearby. It wasn't long before he began to show off a few sleight-of-hand card tricks. A shell game soon followed, though Sherpa never kept any of the money he won, choosing instead to return it to the passing businessmen, beat cops, and children he conned so cheerfully at his new sidewalk cove located halfway between the mansion and the Peacock suite.

With Sherpa content in his middle ground, and Margaret gladdened by his contentment, it was only Robert that continued to struggle. As I said, the Morpho shows were taking an unhealthy toll on his body and upon his mind. The presence of the viperish Fraulein Graf only exacerbated the situation. It was a thoroughly unwell Rouncival that sought in mid-April to escape his woes with an evening alone at the Cort Theatre.

Who can tell what Rouncival expected of that evening? He almost certainly had no knowledge of or about *Uncle Vanya*, and he may hardly have known who Chekhov was either. In all likelihood, he merely wished to partake of the hubbub surrounding Miss Gish's appearance, though his own appearance was made quietly and without any fuss. Perhaps it was just that: for the first time in years, Rouncival was simply the innocuous member of an anonymous audience that made the play such a revelation for him. Perhaps, as the curtain fell, Robert was allowed to forget for a time who he was as both he and his Sachem doppelganger were swept away by Miss Gish's fabulous wake. Perhaps it was the drama itself—so full of longing and indolence, a play both hazy in atmosphere yet possessed with such clarity—that somehow lanced Robert's wounds and made him see other possibilities even in his misery. Perhaps it was merely that such a star of the silver screen had stepped down, into the real stage of the world, and performed so admirably that set Robert in a new direction. Perhaps by falling in love with the stage again, Rouncival realized how perverse his relationship to the footlights had become. We have a slight confirmation of these conjectures through a recording Rouncival made in the study sometime during the '30s. At great expense, he had a device hidden behind the study walls wherein he could tape his own voice. Like many toys, the device was hardly ever used, but a couple recordings are still extant. Though this cassette is obviously not the original tape, here is a quite drunken Robert describing that evening at the Cort Theatre.

Ahem. In the name of posterity, I have a short thing I'd like you to hear. Really, it's not much. And I do hope this finds you [sound of fumbling, something being dropped] Goddamnit! Well, we're off to a flying start, eh? Hah. Us and Lindbergh, I suppose. That jackass. I've walked on air four nights a week, stepped through walls, and then made the walls bleed, but no one's ever hopped in my name. Such a hop it would be, right? Alas. Hehheh.

Funny, but this machine makes a person want to sing. I'll refrain. Oh, what the hell. April in . . . Well, it's April in New York at least. Or it was then. Then being what I wanted to tell you about.

Have I told you I hope you are well? I do mean that. Has been so long. Of course . . . well, no matter.

Let's keep it straight, huh, boys? [affecting deeper, rolling voice] "Just 'cause it's show business doesn't mean this is monkey business!" Barnabas, you fool, you. Could have been the best show manager either side of the Mississippi, would have had five rings under your whip. Instead, you ran an asylum and always hired wastrels, waifs, and hacks like myself. Here's mud in your eye, Barnabas.

How do I get this thing . . . Oh, it's still running. Here, just let me help myself, heh. Back to the beginning now. C'mon, Robert, the curtain is up, time to give the guns their fodder. All right, it was April. I'd just seen Lillian Gish. Hot damn, what a woman! Part cherub, part Mata Hari. Lord, and the get-ups they were wearing. It was a Russian play that night, Uncle Vanya. Naw, I don't know either, I just went to see Gish. First time out of the movies and into a real show in god knows how long. Too tired to do anything else. Leg like red ants had built a hill under my knee. Kept stretching, trying to get comfy once I was seated. Booted some old matron in the back. Biddy turned and gave me the eye, I scowled and grabbed my balls, told her doctor's orders. Hah. Then kinda wondered if I was going to get the boot from the usher when she got up and left. Didn't care, just wanted to stretch my leg, only empty seat in the house, saved like on purpose for my leg.

Goddamn, I don't know. I was so tired that night. And the rain and all. I hardly heard anything they said up on stage, I could just tell everyone was down and out despite their fancy digs. Yeah, tell me all about it. I thought at intermission, a quick stroll outside, a puff on the pipe, back in, didn't even bother with the lobby scene. Knew half of them in there, hated half of that crew anyway. You might have liked them, though, maybe your kind of crowd. Airs and honor and all. Fuck 'em. My leg hurt.

That last act, though. Maybe it was the smoke and all, maybe I just fell asleep for a while. Barely remember, to be honest. Actors crying, actors stretching, actors complaining about being bored, wanting to go to the city, but everyone nice about it, though. Like,

"Yeah, buddy, this is how it is. Want another slug of the Czar's finest?" But when I woke up, alone it felt, all those faces turned up towards the stage. I felt like I was on a raft, floating backwards, away from the tide, and damn it felt good. And there on stage was Lillian Gish, hot damn what a woman, taking her bows far in the distance and I realized the audience was applauding, I'd thought it was waves or something. I didn't know whether I was coming or going, but it felt fine either way. That theater, what a place, fancy and sort of sad just like the play. I didn't want to leave. I just wanted to watch, to stay there, floating around on my little raft, my leg up on a set, and let the waves carry me home.

After that, no way I was going back to that sour bitch at the Peacock. Another night of that . . . No way in hell. Hailed a cab, told 'em to take me downtown, down where the lights don't shine so bright. Told them to take me into the Bowery and I gave them a street name. The hack didn't want to do it but a Ben Franklin changed his tune. Watched the rain come down, thought about Gish, thought abut how nice it was to be in a cab in the dark, not going anywhere especially except maybe even down to the Battery, to get off this island and out to sea. Wasn't long before the cab stopped, though, and there it was, like always, the Half-Shell. I laid another Ben Franklin on the hack and told him to get some sleep. "You too, mister," he said. "You look like you could use some." The lights like always were on in the Palace, shadows at the check-in, and then I breathed, taking in the rain and the April air and the darkness on the streets. Felt good.

Felt even better to finally let myself stumble through the saloon doors, almost falling really, just so tired and worn down with my leg and all. Silver, like always, grabbing me, getting me into a chair, the black cat, tea, what have you, and I told him, "Bill, we *gotta talk. I just gotta talk." And he listened, and that's how I came to the decision to leave the life behind for a while, to go back home. I was just too tired to walk on air anymore. I hope you're well. Why don't you write more often? I'm always at home, you know. Hah. Old fuddydud Robert. Always at home, [noises, mutters, tape ends]*

It is impossible to know whom Robert intended this recording for. Whether it was an anonymous audience, Tillinghast, Ellstein, or perhaps even the ghost of his brother, we'll never know for sure. Either way, as you can tell, Robert emerged from the Cort a newborn man. And as always, whether in a state of crisis or swelling confidence, Rouncival sought out Bill Silver. He found the old man dozing behind the Half-Shell counter and together they stayed up the entire night. Robert broke down, confessing that he was at the end of his rope, that he could no longer perform as the Sachem, that the shows were quite literally killing him. Silver listened and listened, for a while taking Robert close and holding him as Rouncival sobbed, wracked by a lifetime of travels, illusions, heartbreaks, strains, and homelessness.

As Robert pulled himself together, he sat at the counter, and soon Bear the cat came out, bonking Rouncival happily. He still recognized the magician, and as Robert stroked the black cat, he knew what he had to do: he had to go home, or as close to there as possible. The city and the stage had given him much, and he had certainly returned the favor, but it was time to step off. He would cultivate his own garden, so to speak, and even if still miserable, he would be so in a manner befitting the depressed dignity of *Uncle Vanya*. Wiping his tears away and still rubbing the cat, Robert told Silver, "I too am from the Old World. Now, I have to go back." Silver held his hands together, praised God, and grinned, "I told you, you shouldn't have sold that house! Didn't I tell you that?" If the Sachem Morpho was no more, then Robert "The Great" was no more as well as Rouncival resolved to move upstate, away from the limelight. Aside from the very occasional lecture here in the study, whether he would ever perform again was very much in doubt.

One more note on the desk. After procuring the pieces so underhandedly, Rouncival always hoped he would receive a letter from the Soviet dictator regarding the essentially stolen desk. Alas, Stalin was too busy purging generals and deliberately causing famine in the Ukraine to bother dropping Robert a note. Robert would lightly chasten friends when telling of his hopes, "In my heyday, that red thug would have come hat in hand to the back door, begging to discuss the matter, and he'd have been lucky to get a foot in. Now, it seems I'm off the tyrant A-list." Then he would laugh and laugh at his own little joke.

THREE

The little man with the touch of grey at

his temples bowed quietly, still with that

imperturbable smile. And the crowd cheered

him again, before it began slowly to dissolve.

—Pittsburgh's *The Sun*, reviewing Houdini's

escape from a straitjacket

THE
Sword
OF
Sherpa

Continuing my own, ah, slight tyranny, please come this way. Yes, right here in front of the large window. If you will all look up, you'll see what appears at a casual glance to be a rather odd set of hanging chimes. Yes, yes, young sir, you have a sharp eye: indeed, that is a knife in the center of the group. It is surrounded by a number of worn-down handles and hilts, none of which are remotely close in quality to the work of the arms makers of Seville. This chiming set of knives and broken handles, what Rouncival would call "the sword of Damocles," is in fact Sherpa's knife surrounded by all the hilts he'd ever hand fashioned for it. As such, it is one of the most treasured objects in the study. That Robert would refer to the blade that saved his life in the context of Damocles says much about Rouncival. The legend of the sword of Damocles originates in Greek myth, when the courtier Damocles told his king, named Dionysius the Elder, that power must be a great joy. Later, Damocles was invited to sit on the throne himself, where he realized an immense sword was suspended above his head by a single horsehair. Placed as such by Dionysius himself, the sword was intended to be a reminder to the courtier of the precariousness of life and power. I shall leave it up to you, good people, to decide how Robert and Sherpa's relationship parallels that legendary mold.

As I was telling you before, Rouncival had finally called it a day. The Sachem Morpho shows were blessedly ended, and Rouncival spent much of the summer of 1930 looking for a country house. Though he still resided at the Peacock, his affair with Hilary Graf was also mercifully concluded, though "mercy" would hardly be the word to describe the final scene. Rouncival simply ordered Graf to leave the suite immediately, telling her if she was not out by the time he returned from purchasing a newspaper downstairs, he would call the police. Of course, Miss Graf protested most vociferously, demanding to know what had changed, but Robert would hear none of it. Instead, he stood at the door, checked the time on his pocket watch, and said, "Ten minutes. If you're here when I return, I'll probably kill you." The last that was seen of Miss Graf at the Peacock Hotel was her sobbing in the lobby, a few negligees plus a red tasseled lamp in hand as she fled Robert's wrath.

With Silver now as his consultant—sensing Graf's fascist, anti-Semitic leanings, the old man had refused to even be in the same room with the Prussian—Robert spent his days scanning real estate advertisements and remaining, for the most part, sober. With Silver a constant presence, he dared not drink before noon or light his water pipe in front of the old man. Whenever Rouncival did indulge in Silver's presence, the old man's tactic was of acting as if nothing untoward was going on, then waiting until Rouncival was exhausted and inebriated before starting in on endless, sharp-tongued harangues. Silver became such a scold that Rouncival kept sober if only to relieve his burning ears. Acting also as Robert's manager, Silver dealt with any and all press inquiries. The newspapermen wanted to know when Rouncival would return, why the cancelled shows, et cetera, and the old man was a maestro, playing the press corps for all its worth. He insisted Robert's retirement was the real thing, but hinting all the while at a possible comeback. Silver proved a good Tammany man still, dodging the tough questions with a nudge and a wink as he kept Rouncival's name in the headlines to ensure options were available no matter what path Robert chose.

Among those who saw such headlines were Margaret and Sherpa. Though both were dubious so far as Robert's actual retirement went, the fact Rouncival had made it plain he was leaving New York City caused mixed feelings. For Margaret, burdened as she was with family concerns, including Uncle Freddy's worsening health, the idea of Robert heading to the mountains like an elder elephant was a relief. For Sherpa, however, the news struck a nerve, and one that Margaret did not comprehend or even know existed for a number of months. Never known for his loquacity, Sherpa became even more aloof, spending most of his hours at the sidewalk cove before taking suddenly to evenings out without Margaret's company. He began to visit his old Bowery haunts, drinking in the saloons of bootleggers before coming home to the mansion very late. Silver even reported to Margaret that he had seen the retired pirate near the Half-Shell one evening, standing in the shadows across the street but never quite able to make himself cross through the swinging doors.

Distraught at her husband's distance and nocturnal proclivities, Tillinghast complained to Blackwood in a letter, "Things are terrible here! When are you coming home? Roberto has become like a stranger, never speaking, out until all hours, and even worse somewhat mean-spirited when he is about the house. I had been warned about the two-year doldrums in a marriage, but a warning hardly makes the situation any better. To be honest, I am furious at him most of the time, and he seems to feel the same towards me. Meanwhile Uncle Freddy is a wreck, dropping by at the oddest of times, coughing and clutching himself but refusing any money or even to go to the hospital, just sitting in Father's old library for hours on end because one chair there is the only place, he claims, that he can sit comfortably anymore. These are the men in my life, Evie! Please, come home, I think one good afternoon of chat at the café, with you setting me straight as always, would be just the ticket." Alas, Miss Blackwood was consumed with her affair with Standish, writing three, sometimes four poems a day as she attempted to purge her own difficulties. Separated by the entirety of America, the two women would be forced to handle their respective woes alone, for better and for worse.

Margaret's sorrow deepened when Uncle Freddy finally passed away in June. He lived to make one final bet, a winner at the last as he picked Gallant Fox to take the Belmont Stakes. The paltry, two-dollar bet was barely a drop in the bucket so far as his debts went, but at least Freddy, a gallant fox himself, passed from this world with a slight smile of contentment on his face. Margaret collected the Phi Beta Kappa pin from his hovel of a flophouse room, then returned home to find that other somewhat gallant fox, Rouncival, had discovered his future den.

It was all over the papers: Rouncival had purchased an old Dutch manor house upstate and was already in the process of arranging the move of his many magical trunks and effects. Rouncival himself was delighted with the find: as you know, the house and the study you are currently standing in is located in the town of Kaatershook, New York, a place Rouncival had seen on many of the local maps as he grew up in nearby Kingston. Though he did not have to return to the grim memories of his childhood home, Kaatershook was quite close enough. The manor, once a summerhouse of the mighty Van Rensselaer family, was tucked in the hills between the river and the secluded yet fully functioning village. With a post office, a small grocery and sundry store, as well as a snuggish tavern called the Old Patroon and the train line to New York also close, most all of Rouncival's needs could be met easily enough, and he paid cash on the barrel for the manor with its run-down atrium. He planned on installing himself at the manor by September latest, and as Silver informed reporters, no, there would not be any going-away shows. The retirement had well and truly begun.

With concrete knowledge of where Rouncival had gone to, Sherpa's behavior became even more erratic as autumn wore on. Twice he actually fleeced businessmen from his street-side card games, refusing to return the monies he had conned, and twice Margaret had to come to the shop to deal with irate police and her standoffish, unapologetic husband. The late-night drinking binges continued, and soon even a few objets d'art from the 5th Avenue mansion began to disappear as Sherpa funded entrances to high-stake poker games. These games were dangerous in the extreme when one considers Sherpa almost certainly used his sleight-of-hand skills to swindle the other players, all of whom were wealthy and powerful men with many means at their disposal. Knife at his side or no, Sherpa in all likelihood would have been a dead man if the others had caught wind of his sharping. The risk was the reward, though, as Sherpa continued to chance his life on a marked spade or a jack up the sleeve. Slowly but surely, Margaret's husband fell dangerously into his old, waterfront ways. In early December, a very desperate Margaret confronted her husband. As always, we have the Blackwood correspondence to thank for knowing what was said that cold, drizzly evening.

Evie, you know how this house is. God knows I've tried to make it as much of a home as possible, but the thoughts of Mother, Father, and now poor old Freddy seem to take up most of my mind, where they rattle and rattle around like so many Marleys on Christmas Eve. Last night was the worst of my recent hauntings. Roberto was out, like always, god knows where and doing god knows what (two more Dresden figurines gone from the sideboard recently!) and I was alone, like always, watching the rain and sleet. I thought I was going to go out of my mind. Every time the wind gusted into the panes I just about leapt from my skin. It wasn't long before I'd gone into the cellar and opened one of Father's vintage reds, and it wasn't long after that I was down there again, selecting another. The wind seemed to be everywhere at once, banging all around the windows and the eaves, and finally I sat with the bottle and the glass in Freddy's "good chair," too scared and, yes, too soused to move anymore. That's when Roberto came home, and Evie, oh boy, I let him have it.

By the time he found me in Father's library, I was good and worked up, and before he'd even shed his drenched coat or taken off that damn felt hat I lit into him. He just stood there, blinking and wiping rain off his face as I cursed and shouted and stormed about the room like a Fury. I called him a thief and a drunk and a liar and a cheat and dared him to explain himself. I told him I thought I was going insane, that I was alone all the time, that I was running half the industry of America but couldn't get my own husband to sit down for even one dinner a week. I told him I was abandoned and angry, and that I couldn't and wouldn't put up with him running around at all hours with who knows what whores sitting in his lap, though honestly that's the one thing I don't believe he has done. I didn't care, though, I might have accused him of being part of the Lindbergh kidnapping, it just didn't matter anymore.

And then, of course, Robert came into it. I told him, "You think I haven't noticed? You think I'm an idiot? Ever since that bastard, the one who sold us down the river despite all we did for him, the one who never offered a word of thanks or respect or anything at all, the one who couldn't come to Freddy's funeral or even send flowers despite all the money Freddy made for him, who said those evil, evil things to poor Evie, the one who fired you even though you saved his life, you think I haven't noticed that ever since that creep left town you've been another person? What? What is it with you two? No, I don't even care about Robert, what is it with you? Tell me now or so help me god, I do not know what I will do."

Evie, as soon as I said that last part I regretted it. I couldn't believe my own words. The last thing, the last thing I want in the world is to be apart from Roberto. I don't know, though, somehow it just came out, and then I was so, so scared. I thought, If he truly doesn't love me anymore, I'm going to find out right now and then I think I am going to kill myself. Not tonight, I can't bear such a thing, not this night with the wind and all, this night such a thing will kill me.

Roberto just stood there, shaking he was so angry. I could literally see his nostrils flare, and I knew his Spaniard's blood was up. He walked towards me, his fists clenched, those brown eyes so cold and huge, the water still dripping down his face, and I shrank back into the chair. I think I sort of gasped something like, "Oh, please, Roberto, I didn't ..." but it was too late. He drew that knife of his, that goddamned knife, and raised it up. I can now say what it feels like to believe one is about to be murdered by one's lover, and it feels like nothing. The drain has been pulled, and everything, your life, your thoughts, words, all except the fear goes down the pipes. It is a vacuum. All I could do was put my head down, saying (I think) over and over, "Please, please, Roberto ..."

I could smell the rain coming off his shirt as he raised his arm. I think I could smell the fury, the sweat, all of it. Then I felt the rush of his arm coming down with that terrible knife and heard some sort of thud. I thought, "My god, I have been stabbed and it sounds like a thud, and it doesn't hurt at all. Will it hurt before I die? I hope not."

But then I opened my eyes and saw the knife quivering in the table next to my chair. I looked up, into Roberto's face, and instead of rain it was tears running down his cheeks, and I swear the tears were as black as his hair. Then he said so quietly, so thickly, as though he'd been trying to say it for all of his life, "Cuando yo soy Sherpa, yo no soy Roberto!" And as I blinked back my own tears, I understood, Evie, I understood at last, and it was all so simple. Of course: if he was Sherpa, he could not be Roberto, and I reached out, slowly, then firmly, and laid my head against his stomach and held him as he just stood there, exhaling and trying to catch his breath. I swear, I could feel the scars beneath his wet shirt and I knew, I knew at last what he had gone through to become a decent man, the man I knew and the man I married. Of course, I've known all along about him and the Caribbean, his past and all that, and of course I'd always found that part of his allure but never before had it sunk in. I just held him and then he held me, his rough hands on my shoulders, and I thought of him so long ago but not that distant either, as a pirate of some sort, as a cruel man, a bad man, a man who truly was a thief and a cheat, who took from those who had even less than he did. And I thought also of far worse things, that he had killed men, killed them, Evie, and left their bones for gulls, that he'd taken women who did not want to be taken, and left them too, bloody bones alone beneath their rape, to the docks and buzzards and bestial people who prey upon such women. I thought of all that, of how he saved Robert so long ago, of why he did it and how such a thing, the seemingly random decision to be a savior rather than a destroyer, had changed his whole life, that everything rested on where his knife was plunged, and once the decision had been made, he could not go back, that as long as he had Robert, a cripple and a genius and a creep and Judas and so many other things beside to protect he could not become what he once was: Roberto the bad man. Instead, he was Sherpa the Silent, Sherpa the Protector, but without Robert . . .

And as we clutched each other, tighter and tighter, I whispered into his scars, "I know, baby, I know . . ." and it was more than that, it was myself that I knew too, that I needed that bastard Rouncival as much as he did, that none of us could be anything like what we wanted to be without him. That when I was Minnie the Pearl, a flounce and a floozie and an escape artist whose breasts themselves cracked wise, I was not simply a Tillinghast, a Wampum heiress to blood money and madness and war mongering. Somehow he had transformed all of us with his cheap il-

lusions and rude ways, made all three of us his partners forever whether he was grateful or even aware of the fact. Whether he could have been "Robert the Great" without us I'll never know, but I did know at that moment, holding my dear husband with a knife stuck in the table next to us, that Robert, for all his wrongs, is the only one of us ever who called himself "Great." Maybe it's simply that we need a wizard to help us escape the dungeons and chains of our lives, and Robert, damn him, is the only one we've got.

So I held my husband (to call him Sherpa seems strange but it's the way it has to be, I cannot ever, after last night, call him Roberto again) and looked into his eyes and asked, "What shall we do? Just tell me, we can do anything. What can we do?" and he sighed as though a great weight had been lifted and pulled a dripping ad of some kind from his back pocket. It was folded so many times, he'd obviously been holding onto it for some while, and he unfolded it for me to read. It was a real estate advertisement, for a house in the country in a town I'd never heard of before, but I knew, knew somehow it was close to Robert's new home, and I took his hand and closed his fist around the ad for whatever godforsaken house that is and told him, "Of course, of course, as soon as we can, we'll go there. As soon as we can, oh my sweet baby, I promise . . ."

Indeed, the house Sherpa had found the advertisement for was less than two miles as the crow flies from Robert's manor. It only took six weeks for Margaret to arrange purchase of the house, a modest yet elegant structure of the late Federal period, as well as the subsequent move. The end of those six weeks revealed another change in the couple's life together: Margaret was pregnant. She herself always believed the child was conceived that dark, icy night in the library, and who are we to doubt? Amidst all the death and suffering she had seen the previous years, the expectation of a child was a source of great hope for Tillinghast, and it was with a quietly light heart that she and Sherpa came upstate to be near Rouncival. Tillinghast settled into the new abode swiftly, making plans for the baby and still running her empire through three telephone lines installed at great, great expense in the "cottage," as she and Sherpa referred to their home in the country.

The cottage, now an ice cream parlor that I am sure many of you know quite well for its delicious, homemade peach flavors, was less than two miles from Robert as the sherpa walks, so to speak. Hernandez took to crossing the lovely fields, pastures, and wooded lots to sneak looks at Rouncival's manor and, we must assume, Robert himself. Though unseen and not making his presence known, Sherpa continued to watch over the magician, often from that line of white pines you can see so clearly from the windows right there. In fact, later, one of the child's earliest memories would be of being carried on his father's shoulders across a field of summer hay, down a leafy ravine and back up the other side again, to stand hidden in the pines as his father waited for the lights to dim in the great house across the firefly-lit lawns. For many years, that walk would be a mystery to the child, almost a dream more than a memory, a dreaminess enhanced by his being carried half-asleep back through the darkness of the fields to find himself awake again, his mother touching his cheek, in the mothed light of the front porch.

Now, as we take one last look at Sherpa's knife hanging above our own heads, I can tell you the knife wasn't hung there until quite a few years later, during the final days of Robert's illness. The two old friends had spent the evening here in the study, drinking and reminiscing, and by the end of the session, Sherpa had fetched from a box his knife and its many broken handles. Whatever Damoclean import the blade had for Robert or for Sherpa, still, after cutting themselves and clasping hands, in many ways we can think of the hanging of the knife as the last illusion those two blood brothers would ever concoct together.

A

Trunk

O F

Wonders

Yes, the afternoon is wearing on. I assure you, there are not too many more exhibits. For better or for worse, Robert's untimely death keeps the tour, as well as, haha, my own loquaciousness, to a limit. If you would, though, this way, past the potted palms— yes, madam, a nod indeed to Sherpa's fondness for such—and the small orange tree so as to not finish the tour in the gloaming. I would not suggest trying the taste of those oranges, young sir: while quite pretty, their tiny size belies the sourness of the fruit. Atrium or not, a study in upstate New York will never quite be suitable as an orangerie.

Now, as you can see, this magnificent trunk, emblazoned so artfully with Rouncival's name and several cross-boned skulls, is in fact Robert's magical trunk. It is rather typical of any made during the period, with numerous hidden chambers, false walls and compartments, et cetera. It is also the trunk that Tillinghast, as Minnie the Pearl, loved so to escape from. During construction of the study, however, its use was much more mundane. If you will allow me, and no, do not fear standing too close, nothing whatsoever is going to jump out at you, you can see in fact the trunk contains mostly odds and ends, as well as a sheaf of receipts and notes. Not so different from any string-and-pin drawers found in our own homes, eh? Rouncival, like all of us, simply needed a place to store his many loose ends as the study was being built.

Considering the man, though, the receipts, correspondences, and other un-categorizables are a keen look into how the study was actually designed and filled with the wondrous objects surrounding us. And what Robert did not actually keep in the trunk has been added to by his estate's subsequent researches, as the trunk continues to be a depository of all artifacts related to the study's construction. Certain elements of the trunk have remained, for the most part, untouched; here, you see a small compartment where Rouncival stored a mass ball of twine. Ha, yes, even the great magician himself needed a place to keep twine for a rainy day. Other objects, however, are far more revealing. We shall take a look at just a few of these and perhaps, in our own minds, watch the study build itself around us.

Before we explore the trunk, though, I should preface these finds with a bit of background information. Really, there is very little to say regarding either Robert or Margaret and Sherpa during this period. From late 1930 until 1933, both sides were enmeshed in their own projects. While Robert was busy creating a museum, some say even a mausoleum, for himself, Sherpa and Margaret were equally consumed with the raising of their son. After a very difficult birth, and one that would require Margaret not ever again attempting to have children, a son came into this world in mid-September 1931. Tillinghast very nearly paid for the child with her life, but fortunately for all, the local doctor was far better than the one that misset Rouncival's broken leg so many years before. Nevertheless, it was touch and go for a while, with Sherpa lurking next to the bed the whole time. Who knows, it may have been his presence, knife included, that made the physician so determined to stave off disaster. All in all, Margaret recovered from the ordeal of the breach in good spirits and fine fettle, and the boy, named Juan, was a joy to both her and Sherpa. Though the Great Depression was nearing its desultory climax, one would never have known it at the cottage, as the mother suckled the child, phones in both hands as she kept the Wampum empire steady on course. Sherpa, when not assisting with the child, took to the outdoors, fishing for trout in nearby streams and, as I said, keeping silent vigil on Robert's progress. Though Margaret was not overjoyed with her husband sneaking off to the woods surrounding Rouncival's mansion, she let things be, knowing all too well how dangerous the alternative was.

There was one sorrow in Margaret's heart, however, when she learned of Evelyn Blackwood's suicide in October, 1932. Much as Robert was forced to read his own words following the death of his brother, so too was Margaret offered such a cold comfort when Blackwood willed the entirety of their correspondence to her. The inheritance also included one unsent note that said simply, "I understand now what you meant when you spoke of the vacuum of the soul when faced with murder by one's lover. In this case it is my own face in the mirror that causes all to drain away, to some place empty and echoless. I have been so stupid, and I am so ashamed. Maggie, I am sorry. I am going to follow that tide down, down to where an end to this, if nothing else, exists." Understandably, Tillinghast went into a period of deep mourning, a period curtailed only somewhat by the presence of her son and the solicitous care of Sherpa.

Though feeling relatively unburdened for the first time in years, Rouncival soon discovered that an automobile would be a great assistance when living in the country, and he purchased for himself a 1930 model 7-45 Roadster. Yes, yes, it is the same automobile you saw parked in front of the manor, and yes, I agree completely, officer, an amazing machine. With the apple red color, swooping black details, fawn drop top, and whitewall tires, it is, and was, a showcase automobile. It certainly must have created an impression as Robert drove, often at a very high speed, from one end of the county to the other in search of hidden lanes, back country curves, and shaded parking places near the many small ponds and lakes that bless this area. Rouncival even did away with his traditionally funereal dressing style, choosing instead to bedeck himself in tweeds and cream trousers, and he must have appeared quite the country squire as he motored throughout the countryside. No doubt the residents of Kaatershook were bemused as their new neighbor roared past in his Roadster. If they had known of the bottle of gin he kept perpetually iced in the passenger seat, they may not have been so sanguine regarding his speed.

Robert, for his part, hardly cared at all what the neighbors thought. So long as he was served in a timely fashion at the Old

Patroon—open despite Prohibition due to an unholy alliance between the owner of the tavern, the county sheriff, and whoever controlled the upstate bootlegging operations, be it Dutch Schultz or his rival, Legs Diamond—Rouncival was more than content with his environs. When he felt the need for company, he always had the Roadster close at hand, and if he didn't he honored his own time-honored tradition by hanging his top hat on the knob of the front door. If anything, whether maniacally driving or locked up tightly inside the manor, it was planning the study that dominated Rouncival's thoughts.

Which leads us again back to the trunk. Installing the hollow volumes was one of the first and foremost ideas Rouncival had regarding his museum, and it was to *LeClerq and Sons, Decorators and Exporters*, Rue St.-Germain, that he turned to. Why Robert felt he required a Parisian decorator and not one in New York City is a mystery, though a few close to Rouncival at the time said the choice of LeClerq had more to do with a past history of other dealings, namely opium smuggled to Rouncival via Marseilles and LeClerq's far-flung operations, than it did with the quality of Monsieur LeClerq's skills as an interior designer. Rouncival would continue to indulge in that substance all the way until his death, though by the end the drug of dreams and sleep was far more of an anodyne than it was addiction or source of amusement. Nevertheless, whether LeClerq was Rouncival's sole source of the drug or no, that did not stop Robert from chiding his dealer quite viciously when it came to details of the hollow library. To wit:

LeJerk,

The third shipment of "books" arrived today, and I cannot tell you what a joy I felt at seeing the crates delivered into the study.

Nor can I express to you the dismay I felt when, straw thrown all over the room, I realized you had not followed my directions even in the slightest regarding the titles/authors to be inscribed on the volumes. I understand that perhaps your English is not up to par and that in a man's life many things can occur, such as drunkenness or a sexual escapade which leads towards distraction or maybe even a fall down the stairs, but still, Monsieur, really! This is a botch on scale with Dreyfus, if you'll excuse my allusion to that rather sad episode of history. Where I had asked, actually insisted, no, let me say again, actually paid for volumes in a certain, very deliberate order, with titles such as "Bamboozle the Noose" by Codly Herringbone next to "The Grim Sleeper" by J. A. Scape, instead I receive books by actual authors, all of the horrible type. My god, could you relax in your home (sumptuous I am sure beyond any tax collector's understanding) surrounded by such modern misanthropes as Lewis, Mencken, Wharton, Woolf, Lardner, and Snow? A snow job indeed, Monsieur, with a chill I could dissipate only by burning said volumes in a very large fire in my backyard. If you wish, I could box up the ashes, toss some straw on top, and return the charred order Paris way, but I think we both agree that would be a waste of time for all parties. Besides, I need that straw to put atop grass seed planted where the fire ruined my lawn. You have never failed me in the past, LeClerq, please do not do so in the future.

Yours,

The Rouncival Affaire

As you can tell, despite his relative contentment, Robert had lost none of his bilious wit. When Rouncival's estate was beginning the archival process, *LeClerq and Sons*, still an ongoing and successful operation, were all too glad to rid their records of such poisonous correspondences. There were other, far more pleased notes, however, that seem to confirm LeClerq was in fact still supplying Rouncival with opium.

LeSoot,

Monsieur, you have outdone yourself! First, to find and then deliver to me in such a timely manner Zola's first page is a wonder. But then, upon inspecting the strange bulk of the missive, to find a vial of essence of "agar wood" sent me into a jig of pleasure. Not an easy thing for a man of my type! At the very least, my smile was broad, and broader as the day drifted past in dreamy luxury. I must say, however, your allusion to a being visited by a "person from Porlock" confounded me. As many times as I checked my maps, I could find no Porlock anywhere in the vicinity. I found myself roused and checking the front door every few minutes, wondering who such a man was and why he was going to be bearding me in my own lair. Though effective, a top hat can only stem the flood of guests for so long. I understand you now have no idea what I am referring to either, so consider the favor returned. Either way, bravo, Monsieur LeClerq, bravo. May the ghost of Madame Pompadour make a visitation to your bedchamber this evening and perform as admirably for you as you have done in a slightly different manner for me.

Yours,

Rouncival, Lord of Porlock (Hah!)

I see you smiling and shaking your head, madam. Yes, like Monsieur LeClerq, you are far better read in the classics than Robert was. For those not in on LeClerq's little joke, the "person from Porlock" refers to a remark made by the great Romantic poet Samuel Taylor Coleridge. After, apparently, imbibing of some form of opiate, he fell into a dream, woke, and began to write a poem detailing his vision but was interrupted by a "person from Porlock" before he could complete the work. Perhaps it was best he had such a visitor, for the poem he wrote, "Kubla Khan," remains an enraptured masterpiece of the English language. Indeed, as you can see from the papers in the trunk, Robert was consumed with building his own pleasure dome. Rouncival certainly had a very precise order in mind for the volumes, though again, no meaning has ever been deciphered from the names and titles along the shelves. Like I said, it would have been very typical of Rouncival to create such a dime-store ruse. Despite his wealth and more than insistent attitude, though, Robert was unable to procure every item he wished. Here is one short note sent to Monsieur LeClerq in late 1932.

LeClerq, Sons, or Whoever Answers the Bell
Who do you know in London? Someone, I assume—isn't that the Continental System? Or did that go out with Bonaparte? Foreign currencies have always been a mystery to me. Either way, I have a certain, somewhat grim niche in the study, and I'd like an object associated with the Ripper to place there. Any kind of thing will do, just so long as it has a direct *relevance to old Jack or one of his ladies. What can you do?*
Yours in fraternity, if not liberty or equality,
Rouncival

Thankfully, LeClerq was unable to locate items associated with Jack the Ripper. As I am sure you agree, the lantern niche is horrific enough without any bloodstained additions. Considering Rouncival's often excessive ribbing, it is a wonder LeClerq assisted him at all, but as they say, money makes the world go 'round. One person Robert didn't need to cajole, threaten, or bribe regarding acquisitions for the study was Silver. By mid-1932, much of the study was in place, including the laboriously reproduced Glass Chateau effects, but Rouncival desired a centerpiece for the large room. Struck by inspiration, he contacted Silver and offered a hefty sum for the Silver Stage, seats and all. The germ of an idea regarding a kind of raconteur's club was flickering in Rouncival's mind as well, and having a proper stage, no matter how charred or pitted, appealed to Robert's idiosyncratic idea of a salon. "If the mountain went to Moses," Rouncival wrote Silver, "then a stage can certainly arrive at Robert's. Especially since I'm willing to foot the bill for transport." Wanting to use the carriage house for storage, Silver was glad to be rid of any connection to the theater, and he came upstate to help the workmen reassemble the stage piece by piece within the study.

Besides assisting with the stage, the old man had an additionally tricky task to perform, that of deciding whether or not to inform Rouncival that Margaret and Sherpa were living within a few miles. He suspected that Robert was well aware of their proximity, but Rouncival refused to even approach the subject. Silver was finally forced to blurt the truth, as he and Robert sat in the benches of the just-completed stage set, that he remained close friends with the couple and that they lived a stone's throw away. Robert gazed in silence at the pits in the stage floor, then inquired after Maud and Bear. A stoic regarding his own private life and concerns—in later interviews with the estate, Silver would reveal his lifelong heartbreak that he and Maud never had children of their own—the old man informed Rouncival that Maud had passed away a few months earlier. She had been anemic her entire life and it finally caught up with her. Rouncival was truly and deeply sympathetic for the old man.

They sat quietly for a while longer. Then, typically, Silver brightened somewhat and told Robert he had something for him. Returning with a closed basket from his guest room upstairs, he placed the basket on Robert's lap and told him to open it. Perplexed, Robert did so and out emerged Bear. Old beyond caring, the black cat sniffed and bonked Robert a couple times, then quietly went back to sleep in the basket. Touched in the extreme by Silver's gesture, Robert tried to give the cat back, but Silver, a few tears in his eye, insisted that Robert take care of Bear. "You know," the old man man sniffled, "those damn saloon doors. It's too cold, and with Maud gone and all, I usually sleep upstairs nowadays. It gets too lonely sitting at the counter all night by myself, and there just aren't as many bums and flops around as there used to be. Frankly, the Bowery has gone all to hell, if you ask me, and you know how that old cat enjoys company. Nothing like a good drunk or an out-and-out scamp to liven him up, so invite some people over, would you?" Rouncival caught Silver's drift but still said little.

Ladies and gentlemen, if you would all look towards the bottom of the trunk, you'll see a picnic basket with a quilted blanket inside. Yes, this is indeed Bear's basket. The Old World, such as it was, consisted of this basket beneath the tall windows, where the light could warm the creature no matter what season. Bear continued on in the study for a couple more years and his presence, plus Silver's suggestion of company, formed for Rouncival the seed of the idea for the Harbingers' Club. He would indeed invite many drunks and scamps into his study, and many of them great and famous figures.

Other, even stranger figures would appear following Bear's passing in 1934, though that occurrence was somewhat of a mystery: one afternoon, Robert realized the cat wasn't in the basket.

He searched and searched the entire study, which had been closed and locked at the time, but no sign of Bear was found. Apparently the black cat alone was able to penetrate the Glass Chateau, and Robert believed the beast, like an old elephant, had left for the hills to die on its own. If you look out the window to the far right, you'll see a medieval Irish milepost, from County Limerick in the ancient kingdom of Leinster, marking the cat's ostensible grave. Not long after the cat's passing, Rouncival noticed on Halloween that other cats, numbering in the hundreds, came to the milepost. They sat all night, as black as Bear but with shining yellow and green eyes, high in the oak limbs above the marker. Coincidence or not, Robert was having a party that evening, and the cats in the trees were a marvel to his guests, all of whom thought it was one of Robert's illusions. It wasn't his doing, he explained, but no one believed him. Later that year, or early the next, rather, the same feline phenomenon occurred on Twelfth Night, then again on the eve of Passover, and again still on Midsummer's Night. Proof that Robert had no involvement with this mystery is that the cats continue to do so even now, long past his death. It is truly, truly a mystery to the estate why the cats, harbingers perhaps in their own right, hold vigil on such illustrious holidays. Instead, as with many wonders concerning Rouncival and his life, we choose to accept and appreciate such as part of the natural order of things.

THE

Harbingers' Club

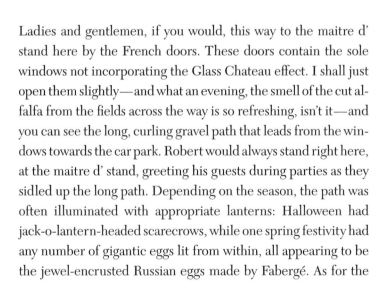

Ladies and gentlemen, if you would, this way to the maitre d'
stand here by the French doors. These doors contain the sole
windows not incorporating the Glass Chateau effect. I shall just
open them slightly—and what an evening, the smell of the cut al-
falfa from the fields across the way is so refreshing, isn't it—and
you can see the long, curling gravel path that leads from the windows towards the car park. Robert would always stand right here,
at the maitre d' stand, greeting his guests during parties as they
sidled up the long path. Depending on the season, the path was
often illuminated with appropriate lanterns: Halloween had
jack-o-lantern-headed scarecrows, while one spring festivity had
any number of gigantic eggs lit from within, all appearing to be
the jewel-encrusted Russian eggs made by Fabergé. As for the

stand, though it came quite cheaply, it is in fact from the famous Delmonico's steakhouse in New York City. Though the restaurant had closed in 1923, its ninety-year history included the invention of such dishes as Chicken a la King and Lobster a la Newburg. Also, during a currency crisis in the Civil War, Delmonico's created and printed its own script, which was good not only at the eatery but at businesses throughout the city as well. Fascinated by the restaurant's audacity, Rouncival sought out the script but had to settle for the stand.

You'll notice as well menus stacked upon the stand, each engraved very carefully. At the top reads "The Harbingers Club," with the date of the meeting and the grinning skull motif directly below. Below that is a menu of the club agenda for that evening. This particular meeting, held in 1934, was highlighted by the presence of H. G. Wells, the noted novelist, Socialist reformer, and one of the first Harbingers' inducted into the club. Below that, you can see that Rouncival is scheduled to speak on "Love, Duress, and Bolsheviks," though the last is in all probability a jibe at Wells and his Socialist penchants.

As if such cuts weren't enough, Rouncival's menus had another, unique aspect to them. When I hold the menu up to the light, suddenly a whole other set of notes and descriptive remarks can be seen. As usual, Robert was up to some rather childish tricks: the invisible text is written in lemon juice, and an illusion any child can perform, though Robert's lemon cure does add another dimension to the trick. The brownish writing also reveals Rouncival's typical gallows humor. The invisible ink beneath Wells reads, "Mr. Wells, in a fit of pique at 'Uncle Joe' Stalin, takes his revenge upon the unsuspecting Harbingers by boring them to reddish tears for upwards of four hours with a lecture on Soviet bolt-making capabilities. The Harbingers, in turn, take their revenge by tossing Wells down a well, telling him it is a time machine." The invisible ink gives such predictions for each member of the club, and by the bottom of the menu, if one reads the secret writing closely, it becomes clear that everyone at the meeting has been murdered before the night is up, including Robert. On this particular night, Rouncival perishes at the hand of a scarecrow, which stuffs Robert with straw before setting his head on fire. That the Harbingers have been "served," so to speak, on the menu has a certain cannibalistic flair to it as well. However dire, though, Robert's lemon-inked forecasts are obviously intended to be a laughing matter.

That Rouncival so heartily enjoyed his guests and the Harbinger parties says much regarding his frame of mind. A secretive, often misanthropic personality during the previous five years, Robert had made a 180-degree turn by early 1934. This was due in part to the completion of the study the year before and Robert's keen joy at acquiring artifacts to fill the room. More likely, though, Robert's contentment can be seen as the end result of his reconciliation with Margaret and Sherpa. The reconciliation, as is often the case with such things, came about from efforts on both sides.

Let me turn back the clock slightly, to 1932. Margaret and Sherpa were happily situated at their cottage, raising their son with all the benefits of a wealthy, countryside upbringing. While Margaret pointedly ignored the fact that Rouncival was living within a few miles of the cottage, Sherpa did not and, as I said, took to crossing the fields and woods to keep a watchful eye on Robert and his doings. As the child grew older, Sherpa began to bring the boy along for his vigils, and together, both hawk-nosed and silent in the seclusion of the pines, they held vigil on the magician. In late 1932, however, twin disasters gripped both parties.

As I mentioned before, it was then that Margaret learned of Evelyn's suicide, and neither child nor husband was able to provide much comfort to her. She descended into depression and sought, when not maintaining her fortune over the phone, to be alone in the cottage. Wanting only to grieve, she was all too glad when Sherpa took his walks and took the boy along with him. As for Rouncival, though happily constructing the study, he soon was laid low by his leg. The years spent on stage, the constant travels, and sleeping in rough quarters had made the leg a chronic problem. LeClerq's smuggled remedies or no, the joints ached terribly every day, and soon blood clots became an additional and constant source of woe. Rouncival spent almost every morning wrapping the grossly swollen leg in hot towels infused with lemon juice merely to be able to walk around. Needless to say, despite the accruing comforts of the study, Rouncival was often in a foul mood, and more and more he took to keeping the top hat on the doorknob for days or weeks on end.

His only regular company was on Wednesdays, when a local woman named Nora Springs came by to clean the manor. Miss Springs was a steady, intelligent, and quietly witty woman born of schoolteachers who had returned to the area from her own teaching position in order to care for an unwell mother. While she did pick up another part-time teaching position in Kaatershook, she did the occasional odd cleaning job to supplement her income, for let us not forget: outside of Robert and Margaret's world of luxury, the rest of America was in the darkest depths of the Depression. A trim, curvaceous lady with an unfashionable abundance of chestnut curls, Nora Springs may have provided more than a clean kitchen: Margaret would later insist the two were lovers all during Robert's years at the manor.

Excuse me, madam, did you say, "They were"? If you don't

mind, how ... ? You are Miss Springs's niece? I am sorry, but I must ask, there weren't any children from that union, correct? Rouncival's estate has never believed ... No, there weren't? Yes, I see, your aunt must indeed have been careful, and I must agree also, Robert was not exactly one to be trusted. Ascertaining whether Robert sired any children has always been one of the estate's primary concerns.

Well, my word, madam. I must thank you as always today. You have enlightened us all. Please allow me just a moment to glance at my notes. The tour is now practically embedded in my mind and on my tongue, but I must confess you have given me a jolt, madam. A jolt indeed. Now where have I put that ... ? I must apologize again for my discombobulation. It is always surprising what a small world it is, especially here in the study.

I think I am ready to continue, and thank you again, madam, for your wonderful confirmation of what the estate has often believed but never quite proved. All right, as I was saying, Margaret was in the blackest of moods and refused almost to venture from the cottage, never mind joining her family hidden in the pines. Out of loneliness, she did take to writing to Silver, but his responses were generally very late in coming and obtuse besides. Tammany had trained their man well, as Silver was clearly reluctant to put anything to paper.

All in all, the family at the cottage had begun to live very different existences by late summer of 1933. Margaret attended business and little else, while Sherpa and the son secretly attended Rouncival. It is perhaps a shame that Margaret did not join their outings. Robert, bored indoors and in too much pain to consider a tour, began to practice illusions upon his lawn, wearing the top hat as a kind of personal jest as he did so. Thus, Sherpa and his son were treated to some of the finest yet indifferent performances of Robert's career. The memories, some of the first of the boy's life, would haunt him forever, as he watched the strange man in the top hat limp through the grounds, one moment turning the waters in a birdbath wine-red, the next conducting a chorus line of fireflies. The child would swear later he watched as Rouncival truly enacted a parliament of birds, the sparrows and jays and chickadees through the grounds arguing and debating each other regarding the repeal of Prohibition. The blue jays, growling like Tammany hacks, shouted the temperance-minded sparrows down, though all the birds in unison hooted their approval when it was announced whiskey would again flow legally through the country. By winter of that year, the human Congress would second the feathery parliament.

Another of the child's early memories of Rouncival was perhaps the most significant. On a dark, rainy day in September, the child was unable to stem a cough. Though his father quickly held a hand over the boy's mouth, it was too late, and the child—luckily born with a tremendous memory for details—could see as the magician turned slowly with his bright, bright eyes and stared into the line of white pines. The boy swore he heard the man in the top hat chuckle, "Hah," then could only stare himself as the magician raised an arm and a stream of thin knives flew upwards from the sleeve. One after another the knives rose towards the low clouds, sharp against the sharp rain, and none of them came down again. The man in the top hat turned and began to limp slowly back towards the French doors. When he reached the manor, he paused and removed the hat, holding it towards the door handles. Then, seeming to consider otherwise, he laughed again and entered the house, hat still in hand, and soon lights throughout the gigantic manor began to blink on, shining warmly in all the windows. Sherpa held the child still a moment longer, then released the boy, but the moment they stepped back into the pines, they heard a rasping noise. Looking closely, they saw all the knives had landed, coming down as one. Blades buried deeply in the soft lawn, the hilts formed an arrow pointing towards the door. Sherpa nodded to himself, and together he and his son crept back to the cottage to tell Margaret of Robert's invitation.

At first, Margaret was in disbelief. That Robert was actually capable of making a conciliatory gesture was out of the realm so far as she was concerned. Sherpa stuck to his guns, however, enlisting the boy's support whenever he could, and after a time Margaret relented. Too tired or depressed to offer much resistance, or enthusiasm either, she simply picked up an umbrella and sighed, "Let's get this over then." All together under a huge, red umbrella, the family took the long way on the road towards Robert's house.

Here, in a note written to Silver that fall—and part of the letters the old man bequeathed to the estate following Robert's death—is Margaret's account of the meeting. It was also her introduction to Rouncival's estate, as well as the study.

It was barely half past five but still, with the rain and all, so dark. I had to blink against the light just to see the lawns as we came upon them, and my god, they seemed to stretch forever. You've told me the manor was nice, but really, that is something you should have stressed. (I know, it's not as if I've met any such news with happiness or even interest, so you're forgiven. This time at least.)

Anyway, I could see the knives in the lawn, and true to Sherpa's word, they clearly pointed towards the door. All the lights were blazing inside, and each of the windows seemed to have a halo of golden mist around its edge. It was truly beautiful, but knowing Robert and all, a beauty I suspected deeply. As we all know, he's pulled stuff (I know you appreciate lady-like manners so I'll spare you the real word I am thinking of here) like this before. Sherpa gave me a wide-eyed look and all I could do was nod. Every squishy step across the lawn made me that much more afraid, and yes, angry at Robert. "This will really be something . . ." I thought, but whether that something was going to be good or bad I had no idea.

By the time we reached the French doors, I was shaking. Sherpa offered to open them for me, but I waved him off and said, "No, you first, in case . . ." The boy in mind, I didn't finish the thought, which was "in case there's a goddamn gun around." Sherpa knew what I was thinking though, and, god bless his courage, it was him that pulled the handles and stepped inside. I folded the umbrella and followed, making sure we flanked Juan.

As soon as I entered that library, I was too stunned to worry about Robert. Again, you told me nothing real about the details of that room, and this time you're not forgiven! My god, what a room. The height of the ceiling alone made my head spin for a second, then, looking around, all those objects, so obviously new and others I recognized with a heartbreak so dear I wanted to cry out. The stage from the carriage, after all these years! And just down the wall, that damn skeleton in the cowboy hat, and across the room what looked like all the furniture from the Peacock! I couldn't believe any of it, and I think I may actually have cried aloud, because far, far away, I heard a cough. Turning quickly and holding Baba's shoulders (and I know I shouldn't still call him that but motherhood sometimes makes imbeciles of us), I squinted and saw Robert for the first time in what seemed like forever. He was sitting on a pile of Persian carpets and pillows, all the way at the other end of the library (since when does Robert read, I'd like to know?), and he had a lemon squeezed dry, sitting on his knee.

It was almost like old times, and I had to swallow hard just to keep from fainting or sobbing. Robert looked so pinched, even with those ridiculous robes and smoking jackets covering him. He's lost weight too, but I could see his eyes, even all the way down there, shining and staring. He was looking at Sherpa. "Oh no you don't," I thought, "there's no way you stupid, stupid men are going to patch this up with a handshake and a drink of whiskey like nothing happened. Not on my watch!" And before I knew it, with every drop of Wampum hubris flowing in my veins, I strode across the room and found myself staring down at Robert as he lounged in his oriental splendor. As obviously sick and pained as he was, he merely gave me a sidelong glance and kept stirring the ice in his drink. That did it. I looked him up and down like I was a mortician inspecting a corpse and sneered coldly, "How's tricks, Robert? From the looks of you, appears like you'll be the bitch in the box this time."

His eyes widened, and I could see he'd lost none of his temper. I felt Sherpa behind me but I waved him back. This was between Robert and me. Robert continued to swirl the ice cubes, but then he looked me straight in the eye and smiled. With his gaunt face and the shadows under his eyes, it was like a skeleton's grin as he pulled back his lips. He started to speak but the voice came from my chest as I heard my boobs say with such quiet happiness, "Oh, Robert, my old friend, it's so good to see you again."

That was truly it, and everything broke inside me. The waterworks started and I could see maybe, just maybe, a tear in Robert's eye as well. It was all so ridiculous, all of it, me and my family scared to death, him half a corpse but dressed like a pasha, *and I threw back my head and laughed. I laughed and laughed, thinking of all the things we'd said and done to each other, of poor, dear Evie and the things he'd said to her, of all the wastelands we'd gone through separately and on our own, and I just couldn't stop laughing because, as strange as it may be, maybe I just needed to hear my own tits talk again. All the blackness of the last year dissipated as I threw myself on Robert, hugging him for all my worth as I whispered into his ear, "Minnie, oh Minnie my pearl, you've come back at last."*

After such a rapturous reception, there were assuredly many drinks and handshakes that evening. Reunited and in each other's good graces at last, the three took to spending much time together in the study, especially with the onset of winter. Rouncival even offered to install extra phone lines so Margaret could work from the manor but she steadfastly refused, denying Robert with a cackle, "There's no way in hell you're going to profit on me by eavesdropping in the hallway. I can just see it now, me whipping open the door and finding you there with a highball glass held to your ear." Margaret continued to run her empire from the cottage, making the occasional trip to New York to quell any boardroom conspiracies and watching the child for most of the day. As for Sherpa, he began to convert a large shed behind the cottage into a workroom of sorts, saying he thought he might open another watch repair shop the coming spring, though Tillinghast strongly suspected he was creating a hideaway for him and Robert to practice new illusions. In the evening, however, it became habit for the family to make the walk down the road, or sometimes through the woods, to Rouncival's. There, with the child put to bed as early as possible in a makeshift bedroom down the hall, they enjoyed themselves quietly, watching the snows fall from the warm expanses of the study. There, they chatted, argued, drank, read the papers aloud, or otherwise sat in silence, forming a kind of harbinger to the Harbingers' Club. All through the winter of 1933–34 the nightly salon met, and once again we have the Silver correspondence to thank for such an intimate glimpse of their very Vanya-esque existence.

Old man, if only you could see us, what a droopy, drowsy group we have become! To think this is Robert "The Great," Sherpa, and Minnie the Pearl, once the bane (or lifeblood) of nightclub owners coast to coast. Even that ancient cat in the basket (Baba loves the thing, they sit and whack each other with their heads for hours on end, I swear) shows more liveliness than us. We yawn, make one kettle of tea after another, read the papers, and let Robert curse whoever or whatever is mentioned as he sits in his oriental tent with joss-embedded candles (I think we all know what that "joss" really is) burning above both ears. With the smoke wreathing his head he looks like Scratch himself. Of course, I doubt Scratch complains as much as him or the rest of us, for that matter: all it takes is a mere chill brushing our faces to send everyone scurrying after an extra sweater or shawl to keep the cold at bay! We are old women, all of us, though I would like to think, even if a bedraggled, in-bed-by-ten hag that I have maintained my figure. Of course, as life has taught me, there are many things I would like to think, and usually I am wrong. Oh well, the study makes short work of such ponderings. Add another dollop of rum to the tea, check Juan to make sure he's asleep, and come back to find Robert, somehow, has turned the frost on the windows a delicious cardinal red!

This is my winter tale, old man, and you'd better take time away from your precious Bowery rascals to write back to this bunch—I promise you, ne'er well is being done up here either.

Love,
Maggie

While historians have often given short shift to the latter Morpho shows, this period at the manor has been positively ignored by most. Here, then, is another look through Margaret's eyes of Rouncival in his lair.

Robert has outdone himself! Today, as I was padding about the manor in fruitless search of some warmer socks, I returned to the study and found Robert slipping something into one of those dratted hollow books on the shelf. The expression on his face was of positive mortification, and I thought, "Oh my, I have to see what he's hiding!" He knew I wanted to find out, and I knew he knew, and the entire afternoon became a waiting game. Rather, it was a contest of bladders, as neither of us would leave the study. I knew the moment I stepped out he'd hide whatever it was in a new place, and he knew I'd pounce as soon as the door shut. Silver, you would have laughed and laughed as we played at nonchalance, all the while crossing and re-crossing our legs and trying not to groan. We become children, and not the well-behaved kind either, when we get together, there's no doubt about that.

Finally, I am proud to say I beat Mr. Great at his own game. Thankfully, he'd been drinking his usual amount (i.e. tremendous quantities of gin) and could stand it no longer. Actually, he could hardly stand at all as he grunted a very foul word and hobbled off for the bathroom. With a little shout of glee I was up to the shelves, pulling that book out, and believe me, I'd kept a close eye on exactly where it was located. I turned the thing upside down and a sheaf of papers fell out. "Good god," I thought, "some kind of secret correspondence!" But on closer inspection, I saw the papers were in fact torn from a book, and were a copy of "Macbeth"! I couldn't believe it, and pulling down the volume next to the first, I saw that one contained "Measure for Measure" plus some poems by Dickinson, all the pages torn from whatever abused real book they'd been in.

Thankfully Robert is even slower than normal these days, and I heard him thumping down the hall long before he reached the study. I re-cached the pages and was well back in my chair by the time he returned. He gave a growl and a glance and went to pour himself another drink. Neither of us deigned to look at the shelves and finally I too rose, needing a pee even worse than before. As I passed Robert, however, I leaned over his chair and whispered quickly, "There's a certain slant of light, especially when one pees at night." He roared and tossed his newspaper at me as I fled cackling, though I damn near wet myself during my triumphant getaway.

Can you imagine—a man of many habits, notably surliness, insobriety, and chicanery, and it is reading—the one good practice he's ever taken up in his life—which he chooses to conceal? Ha, if that isn't Robert for you.

Whether they behaved like old women or rambunctious children, life in the study obviously agreed with all parties. In fact, it agreed to such an extent that as the weather warmed and spring approached, they began to ponder opening their little salon to other guests. Robert, Margaret, and Sherpa began to compile a list of who they knew that might be qualified for an invite, and in turn who they might know as well. It wasn't long before the group in the study—the original Harbingers, one might say—realized that through their widespread connections the possibilities for holding a successful salon were indeed great. It was decided that Robert's midsummer birthday would be an ideal date to set the first meeting. Invites were sent during spring and travel arrangements made for certain of the guests, mostly through the generosity of Margaret; Rouncival refused to spring for either plane or train fares. Though in general it was a rather grandiose party they were planning, still, the invites did declare the occasion to be the first ever meeting of the Harbingers' Club, a moniker coined strangely enough by Sherpa one morning as he was sorting envelopes addressed to the guest list. Robert was immediately captivated with the name, though, and soon enough he was tormenting Margaret and Sherpa alike with his concepts for an actual club. Fortunately for all, they put the kibosh on Robert's plans to have club members sign the charter in blood and other, rather Masonic nonsense. Still, Robert's concept for the menus was met enthusiastically, as was his belief that any official ceremonies or performances should be held upon the Silver Stage. Fortunate also for some was Robert's insistence that anything related to the club be kept in absolute secrecy, including the membership. Once a meeting was called to order, said Rouncival, the Harbingers were then free to do whatever they pleased, without any worries regarding the press or seeing their names in the papers the following day.

As you all know, despite every precaution, the papers did get wind of the party, though the press corps was kept beyond the estate walls, howling for a glimpse of the guests as they pulled beyond the gates in their darkened limos. All in all, the first meeting was a phenomenal success, as the party raged for close to two full days. By the end, extra deliveries of liquor and foodstuffs were being ordered in from Kaatershook, with the limo drivers commissioned to fetch the goods. As one New York gossip sheet reported, "If you were out and about on the town this weekend and noticed a distinct echo in the empty celebrity nightclubs all throughout the city, it's because the stars flocked en masse to the magician Rouncival's country house this weekend and have not been seen since. Your intrepid Man on the Scene was unable to pierce the magician's veil of secrecy, and whether the stars have been turned into doves or toads or are pecking like chickens in a state of hypnosis remains unknown." Margaret was not so purple in her description to Silver of the aftereffects of the party: "It's been four days since Robert's Harbinger party, and I'm still unable to see straight or walk straight or think straight or sleep straight. Need I remind you I am a mother and not so young as I once was? All I can do is mutter from the depths of my crumby bathrobe, 'Never again!' Until next time, of course, and we're already planning on a Halloween bash."

They did indeed plan a bash for All Hallows', and it was this second meeting of the Harbingers—the mysterious gathering of the cats included—that cinched the club's reputation. Once again, strictly secret travel arrangements were made, though it was following this second meeting that, according to the minutes, Frida Kahlo suggested that if certain Harbingers were unable to attend the meeting, nevertheless perhaps they might be able to send work, speeches, et cetera, for perusal if they wished to. Rouncival quickly seconded this, and thus future gatherings were enlightened by the words, if not the presence, of such luminaries as William Faulkner as well as the travel writer, novelist, and one-time wife of H. G. Wells, Rebecca West. Robert especially was a fan of Faulkner's writing, insisting to certain doubters that Southerners were in fact just as strange in their ways as portrayed by the bard of Oxford, Mississippi. While Rouncival may have fondly recalled the peculiarities of Dixie-born Barnabas Welt, it was probably best for all that he and Faulkner did not engage each other face to face: had those two truculent drunkards actually met, the possibilities for a disastrous disagreement would have been considerable. As it was, both were able to appreciate each other's ornery talents from a safely respectful distance.

Sadly, I am not at liberty to reveal the works read and performed on the Silver Stage, some of which would later be published in altered forms while others, too abrasive, insulting, or flagrantly erotic, would never see the light of day beyond the study. Nor can I list for you the full roll of Harbingers, but I will add that aside from those mentioned before, there was a strong likelihood such persons as Charlie Chaplin, George Orwell, Dorothy Parker, Charlie Parker, Dorothy Sayers, C. S. Lewis, Josephine Baker, Joseph Mitchell, Pablo Picasso, Albert Einstein, Thornton Wilder, Erich Maria Remarque, Mary Pickford, Langston Hughes, and Babe Ruth attended a club meeting at one time or another, often under the most hush-hush of arrangements. I can also hint that after much discussion it was decided Salvador Dalí should be kept out despite his multiple, vociferous entreaties. A histrionic attempt to crash one of the parties did not help his cause. To be selected as a Harbinger was a difficult accomplishment, and in the end, it was Roza Ellstein and Roza alone who was ever put on record as refusing membership.

Dalí or no, the Harbingers' Club was truly a salon for the ages. Lasting well beyond Rouncival's untimely death, I can say that even today there may be a Harbinger or two amongst us. Sadly for all, Robert did not live to see his club survive and even thrive decades beyond the founding. In fact, by 1936, he was hardly able to attend meetings himself, and the location of the parties had to be changed. The last time the Harbingers ever met in the study was on Robert's birthday in June 1936. Robert himself seemed to know the end was near. For one, using the device concealed behind the wall of the hollow library, Robert actually recorded a certain portion of the meeting. As you'll be able to tell from the clinking of glasses and raucous background noise, this was most certainly taped during the wee hours of the party. Though I have, for personal reasons, many misgivings about playing you this tape, perhaps just a quick listen is in order for the sake of the tour. Just let me press the button . . .

. . . *Harry, Harry, down here! . . . My god, I can't even tell you how long . . . Would someone, please, get me another lime! What in the world? . . . I'd ask you to dance but my feet seem to be encased in scotch . . . Haha, very funny, Robert, if I'd have wanted a tail I'd have grown one last year after the divorce, you know, to match my cloven hooves and all . . . What beastly people . . . Is that? It couldn't be . . . Charlie, remove your hand from my ass just long enough to get me my drink . . . Who turned off the lights? . . . Keep 'em off! . . . Where'd that cocker spaniel come from . . . ? Rita, how many times have I told you, Boston isn't a city, it's a college, come to New York . . . Please, please tell me that wasn't a gunshot? It wasn't if that will make you feel better . . . Sometimes, Billie, it's so hard, I get so lonely I just want to die . . . Baby, come here . . . I saw him twice, first in Chicago and then in St. Louis, and each time he insisted we still call him "Your Honor" . . . What a fucking whore . . . Okay, where's that hand when I need it . . . Dangerfield! Dangerfield, over here! . . . I saw them out in the bushes, and he was still wearing those yellow sun shades! . . . I'm telling you, when Harding got the nomination he shot himself. He should have shot Harding . . . Oh, do shut up . . . They broke the mold with him, and thank Christ for that . . . Is that Maggie? She's gained weight . . . So have you, darling . . . only in the tits . . . tat for tit . . . has anyone seen my doggy? . . . Yeah, Robby changed him into a partridge and he flew flew flew away . . . I hate you . . . I'd give a million dollars to fuck him naked, even once . . . I'd give ten dollars to screw you clothed . . . That's cruel . . . Whenever I remember that I own a bank, it makes me laugh like a bastard— can you imagine, me owning a bank? . . . You have such lovely eyes . . . Thank you, I got them in Piccadilly Circus on a rainy Wednesday during the war . . . Two words: digestive biscuits . . . That's the most beautiful thing I have ever heard . . . If you're talking about your novel again, I'm going to leave . . . I think she went upstairs to cry . . . Sometimes I imagine my hair is blue . . . That's sad . . . If you were a knight of the Round Table, who would you be? The one that killed Custer . . . All for one and one for ass! . . . Right here? Later, honey . . . Distance makes the heart grow fonder. So do diamonds, boyo, so do diamonds . . . Has anyone seen my dog? Yes, he went up the chimney like St. Nick, arf arf . . . How wonderful for you . . . Stop staring at me . . . We did go to Dartmouth together! . . . I can't . . . Professor Roach, what a grind . . . Please, stop . . . What's your name? . . . I aced that bastard and spent the rest of summer in Rome . . . I won't tell you . . . Please . . . Mussolini and all, what a disaster . . . Okay, but not here . . . Anywhere, just so I can be with you . . . Okay, but not here . . . arf arf arf . . . Turn them off and keep them off, can't you see this is a party! . . . Anywhere . . . Good god, let's go . . .*

I shall leave it up to you to guess whose voices are whose. I have also another rather more sorrowful indication that Robert knew it might be his last party. Here is a short note written to Margaret that summer from one of the guests describing their good-bye look at the study.

Maggie, thank you, as always, for such a wonderful party. A month later and I remain star struck, and you know I'm no novice to the constellations. What I can't get out of my mind, however, was a very strange scene when I finally took my leave. My "companion" and I were walking towards the car, staggering is more like it really, and we were talking about how pinched and thin Robert has looked since the accident. I guess we'd reached that maudlin, exhausted point of a party, the sun was coming up, the sky was just beginning to blue the night away, and a kind of desolation took both of us. Then, reaching the car, I dropped the keys in my stupor and reaching down I happened to look back towards the study. But the study was gone! The whole manor was gone! Instead, it seemed as if all the trees nearby had come to block the view, their limbs linked as they surrounded the house. I sort of choked and my companion turned to see what was the matter. Then she gasped too, and I could see her face pull in, so dark even in the dawn. As you know, neither she nor I are strangers to the stage, and I think both of us were struck with the same glum image of the forest marching towards Macbeth. She whispered sadly, "Birnam Wood is come . . ." and we drove off feeling pretty down and out, thinking of Robert (and yourself) as the forest closed in. All our love,

As you can tell, Robert's illusions were obviously benefiting from his new hobby of reading. The "accident" to which our anonymous Harbinger refers is one of the tragedies of Robert's life. It occurred in the spring of 1936, just when he was pondering a return to the stage. The lectures in the study, as well as the extended applause, had fired his blood again and he was eager to make a splashing comeback. He had a slew of new illusions, none of which he would reveal to anyone, even Sherpa, but he was very excited regarding his projected comeback. "I've brought Hell down upon their heads," he boasted of his stagecraft, "and now I shall give them Heaven they'll never forget." Though Robert would not show his hand, he broadly hinted at some of the illusions he had in mind. With titles like "The Charmed Serpent," "Dance of Seven Vapors," and the intriguing "Field of the Stag King," Rouncival's idiosyncratic Paradise was sure to astound and amaze.

Perhaps thinking overmuch of his future plans, Robert, with Sherpa in tow, drove the Roadster to the Old Patroon Tavern for a springtime revelry. He was going his normal excessive speed when he suddenly clutched at his head and began to slow down. "Funny," he told Sherpa in a faraway voice, "My leg has stopped hurting." Then he fainted and the car careened into a white-blossomed apple orchard. Sherpa, bruised but otherwise uninjured, picked up the bloody, unconscious Rouncival and lifted him from the wreck. No young man himself, Sherpa then cradled Robert in his arms and carried him back to the manor, two miles away. A doctor was called and a diagnosis soon made: Robert had suffered a mild stroke, stemming in all likelihood from one of the many blood clots in his leg. Though Rouncival would regain most of his faculties, he and all around knew his days upon the stage were numbered. Sorrowfully for the world, Robert's vision of Paradise was confined forevermore to the study.

Now, to the back wall of the study. And I do thank you all for your patience. We have certainly run overtime today, and I ask your indulgence for just a while longer as we approach Robert's final days.

This area of the study was in fact one of Rouncival's favorite haunts. In a way, the window, with its view of the lawns sloping down towards the river, was a turnaround for Robert. Following the stroke, Robert attempted to physically rehabilitate himself by pacing from one end of the study to the other, and here at the window was where he rested a moment to catch his breath before turning back again. Like a caged tiger, each day he would pace as long as he, and his leg, could withstand the exercise, which sadly was never for long.

The shelves at this end of the study also became a repository for some of Rouncival's most cherished belongings. Notably, both his father's watch and Robert's opium pipe were placed here each night before he turned in. He would then fetch both first thing every morning as soon as he rose, which was usually very early. The pain in his leg was such that he slept little, and ate even less, and Robert used the watch and the pipe almost as a goad in order to force himself to walk about despite the terrible stiffness and soreness he felt at the start of each day. That such precious objects were used quite literally as spurs was not atypical of Rouncival: pleasure, pain, and a desire for comfort had become one and the same to him.

You will notice also the framed photograph along the top shelf there. If I stretch ... ah, yes, I'm just able to reach it. I seem to remember, haha, having an easier time doing so back in my younger days. Alas, age reduces us in so many ways. Please pass the photograph around so all can get a glimpse. It is the last picture ever taken of Rouncival, and yes, young sir, I agree: he does indeed look "all messed up." As you will all see, his face is gaunt in the extreme, his eyes are pitted, and the shadow of the stroke can be seen in the way one side of his face seems to droop. The ravages of the stroke, the pains in his leg, and undoubtedly his lifestyle also, are plain.

What is not so plain is the magazine he is holding in his hand. If you look closely, you'll see that it is *Life* magazine. Dated November 23, 1936, it is the first ever issue of Henry Luce's groundbreaking photo journal. Wanting to offer Americans an image-centric method of looking at themselves and the world as a whole, Luce created *Life* to immediate acclaim. Robert, like many, was enchanted by the possibilities of the magazine, and the first cover photograph, of the Fort Peck Dam by Margaret Bourke-White, did nothing to harm the sensation. Though it is difficult to tell in our photograph, Bourke-White showed the dam in a decidedly grim light. One monolithic tower rises from another like a series of totalitarian fortresses, all looming heavily above two stooped figures below. The massive concrete towers dwarf the humans, and overall the photo is a stark vision of an impersonal, dryly technological future. Despite it being a dam and ostensibly a provider of power and a better way of life, not a single drop of water can be found anywhere in the image. Struck by the ironies of the cover, Robert posed for the photo and forced an unwilling Tillinghast to snap the picture. She understood full well Robert's intentions for the photo, and did not appreciate the gag. Nevertheless, Robert clearly enjoyed the image of him in all his skeletal glory, smiling as he displayed from his sickbed the premier issue of a magazine emblazoned with the title of *Life*, as he would chuckle at the photo every time he passed by during his morning paces.

Such black humor was a staple of Robert's existence. Aside from it being a sign Rouncival had indeed begun to read in secret, the illusion of the marching forest after the last Harbingers party was an elegant, and frightening, symbol of the claustrophobia Rouncival was feeling. Infuriated that his comeback was being "delayed," to use Robert's euphemism for his condition, he wove his spells in solitary, caught all the while behind the windows of the Glass Chateau. The study, like his father's watch and the pipe, became both a refuge and a cage. Though Margaret, Sherpa, and, increasingly, Nora Springs were around to assist and keep watch over him, truthfully, Rouncival was hardly a pleasant personality most of the time. As before, we have Margaret's letters to a very concerned Silver to thank for giving us a look at Rouncival's last six months. And, madam, I must apologize beforehand: the letter contains a mention of your aunt and Robert's relationship. You do not mind? For all of us, I do thank you for your openness in this matter.

I have to say, not a lot of laughs around here. For one, the heat has all of us in swelter. Even Sherpa, normally like a pig in clover in the warm weather, has grown cranky and short-tempered. (And notice how easily I refer to my ever-loving husband as a swine? Marriage quite agrees with me!) The shutters in the cottage are kept shut tight, and all we do is fan ourselves and snap whenever anyone speaks a word. Just lifting an arm to pour iced tea seems like too much effort. Add on trying to keep Robert fed and moderately content ("hah," as he would say) and I'm sure you can see the jokes aren't exactly piling up.

The only one who seems to have maintained her cool is Nora, god bless her. She accepts Robert's whining and unending grievances with a calmness and stolidity that I find most impressive. In fact, in her own dry way, Nora is quite funny and I wish you'd come up here, old man, and meet her. I know, the Bowery has a ceaseless attraction for you, but here's just a small example of Nora's esprit de corps. Wanting to dig a garden near the far wall of the study, she politely asked Robert for permission before even a single shovel of dirt was turned. Robert, of course, found the suggestion of fresh produce in his yard (and here at last is a laugh: imagine Robert grazing on lettuce at midnight!) completely disagreeable. You'd have thought she'd suggested planting a crop of screaming babies underneath his bedroom window. "There will be no cultivation of crops anywhere on or near my lawn," he raved like that martinet Hitler, adding, "I am hardly the farmer in the dell."

Nora took the abuse in stride and the next day, with Sherpa's help, she raised a grape arbor exactly where she had hoped to have a garden! They did this, and planted the vines as well, while Robert slept, and when he awoke and looked out the window, well, you can imagine. Roars and rants and curses and whatever else. Nora stood the whole of it, and when Robert paused to catch his breath, she merely said, "I can take it down. But I'd hoped we could make our own wine, right here at the manor. It's not quite the Finger Lakes, I know, but . . ." Well, Robert was tickled pink by this idea and imagining I'm sure his own personal, backyard Bordeaux, he gave his fullest blessing. He even takes time now to go out there and check the vines, asking Nora every day whether they need to be watered. Later, I got Nora alone and asked her if the arbor could really make a decent wine. She just gave a shrug and winked, "Well, with Robert tending the vines and all, at least they'll produce a good batch of vinegar." I hooted! She knows her man indeed, and I should add their "cleaning day" continues as ever, and Sherpa and I make sure to steer well clear of the study on Wednesdays.

God bless them both, I suppose, and at least Robert has an appetite for something. He's still losing weight, and has become a picker of plates. Maybe he'll choke down a scrambled egg or two a day, but that, aside from his gin and "joss" ration, is about all. Vinegary anecdotes aside, we are all worried. If you get the chance, please come up for a visit. You're one of the few he'd enjoy seeing, and besides, you can give him grief over the state of his vineyard. That alone is worth the price of admission!

A "vinegary anecdote" certainly. Margaret, despite her worry, was obviously maintaining her own modestly even keel. Another note, written in early September, was not quite so light.

I just wanted to dash off a short thing saying thank you, thank you so much for last weekend. Seeing you did Robert a world of good, and Sherpa and me as well. As soon as you mentioned Davidoff, Robert's eyes lit like I haven't seen them in months. All it took was the memory of one good enemy to get his blood stirring again, though personally I am glad to hear that seemingly hapless man has found his fortune in the world. A string of look-alike "Parisian-style" cafés opened in cities up and down the coast— who'd have thought such a concept could become such a monumental success? I certainly wish I'd have come up with the idea.

At any rate, and not to be a bearer of bad tidings, Robert's condition has gotten much worse during the last week. Gin and lemon soaked or no, the leg is bothering him horribly. The fact he has stopped complaining is ominous, and lately he has been too weary even to whine to Nora or me. The worst, the absolute worst, is when one or the other of us finds him in the kitchen in the morning making his own little breakfast. Robert, cracking eggs with a smudge of flour on his face, can you imagine? He has eaten out, ordered in, or had prepared for him every meal for the last ten years! Now, though, he gets up so, so early. Since both Nora and I have practically moved into the house (and yes, you can be sure cabals abound back at the Wampum boardrooms) we hear him, first thumping down the stairs, then into his study. Back and forth as the sun comes up, then into the kitchen to fix himself a soft-boiled egg or toast. When we go down and tell him just to sit, that we'll make breakfast, he waves us off and says he's fine. He's not, and Nora and I watch, sitting on stools on either side of the huge butcher block, sipping our coffee as Robert dies (oh, I am so sorry, so sorry, but just once I have to say it) right before our eyes. The other day I couldn't stand it and began to cry right at the block. Nora held my hand while Robert hardly seemed to notice, his back to us at the stove as he boiled an egg. Then I felt something like a dry rain at my neck, and Nora's eyes grew wide as she suddenly broke into a grin through her own tears. A silver saltshaker was floating just above me, flicking salt over my shoulder. Robert never looked at us once, just left whistling with his tiny breakfast on a tiny plate, and the saltshaker followed him, floating from the kitchen towards the study. Once he was gone, I truly sobbed and Nora did too, both of us holding hands, trying to wipe tears away, murmuring every once in a while things like "Oh Robert, poor, poor Robert, damn it all, just god damn it . . ."

Such was life at the manor as the autumn continued: an inseparable mix of comedy, tragedy, and enchantment. Coinciding with a flourish of warm weather, Robert's condition improved markedly for a period in mid-October. Enjoying better health and the Indian summer as much as possible, Robert began to visit Sherpa's shed behind the cottage. There, they sat on apple crates, drank cider, and discussed possible illusions for the future. After all the years, they were finally attempting to fashion a buccaneer routine that would actually feature Sherpa as a kind of Blackbeard, lit fuses burning behind his ears as he summoned the Flying Dutchman, Captain Cook's treasure, Leviathan, and a host of other nautical legends from beneath the stage. It was mostly just a pipe dream, as Robert couldn't bear to stand for more than fifteen minutes at a time, but with the sunshine and cider and the warm weather, a pleasant way certainly to pass the ever-shortening afternoons.

The two companions became such a fixture in the shed that Juan, closing in on his sixth birthday, began to sneak out to see what his father and strange friend were up to. Despite a lifelong abhorrence for children, and anything small, actually, Robert quickly made the child a kind of apprentice, showing him how to slip an ace up or down a sleeve or explaining the rudiments of levitation. Then, one day while bringing another jug of cider out to her three men, Margaret came upon the shed even as Juan, laughing til his stomach hurt, was being floated up to the rafters and down again by Robert. Though she enjoyed the spectacle as much as the rest, she also questioned the boy most closely and discovered his apprenticeship when a slew of marked spades slipped to the floor. Turning on the rather sheepish Sherpa and Robert, she told them both, "No way in heck you're sending my son down your crooked path! He's going to go to school and study theology at Harvard. I'll donate ten libraries to get him admitted, I don't care. That way it'll be Harvard's fault if he winds up a thieving rascal, not ours. No more card tricks!"

The card sharping may have ceased but Juan's relationship with Rouncival and the study as a whole did not. Deciding against a public school education, Margaret asked Nora to tutor the boy and she readily agreed. The lessons were held in the study so that Nora could keep an eye on Robert simultaneously. So the boy learned to read from the titles on the hollow volumes, pronouncing the deliberately archaic names and titles as though they were the freshest of words and ideas. He learned his numbers using Rouncival's cancelled checks, and the shape and consistency of the world was taught by spinning Napoleon's marble globe. All the while, Rouncival would surreptitiously teach the rudiments of showmanship, sending Nora on pointless errands with a wink and a nudge so Juan and he could practice stage entrances and how to recover from a flubbed one-liner. Other times, Rouncival sent Juan into fits of giggling by making the carpets and pillows neigh, oink, and moo like barnyard animals. In more reflective moods, Robert revealed to the boy the secrets of the study, explaining each of the objects in turn, sparing the child none of the details as he patted the vaquero on the back and swirled the ice in his glass of gin. The child grew up as much an aspect of the study as the other objects, his untrained mind formed and reformed by the magic and the mysteries surrounding him, all the while basking in the warm light of the windows.

That Indian summer lasted all the way up to Halloween, though the holiday was unusually subdued. For the first time, the Harbingers would meet somewhere other than the study, and Robert, though placid, was obviously dejected. He insisted that Sherpa and Margaret attend the party, held in London that year, but both refused. Instead, all took to the study and had their own gathering, Nora included, waiting for the strike of midnight as if it were New Year's Eve. The cats did not disappoint, appearing at the milepost like always, and the little group watched their green and yellow and orange eyes glisten in the darkness. Even Robert could only shake his head at the spectacle, everyone silent with wondrous fright. It was late that night, long after Margaret and Nora had retired, that Robert and Sherpa became blood brothers and hung Sherpa's knife above the window together.

Not long after that, the weather worsened and so did Robert. The chill rains and sleet make the leg an agony, and no matter what he tried, Rouncival could never make the knee cease its aching. There were no more trips to the shed, as he began to remain in the study most all of every day, even sleeping the night in the Khan's tent. Stairs were often too much for him, as was eating, and he began truly to waste away. Margaret had fresh steaks and seafood delivered daily from New York City's finest butchers and fishmongers, but it was of little use. No matter how she or Nora—a far better chef than Margaret ever was—prepared the meals, they quite literally went to the crows. Robert would hobble to the French doors and sweep his plate into the slush outside, then stand, shivering in his robes as the blackbirds came for their feast. He got an inordinate joy from watching the scavengers wrestle over the scraps, and one day Margaret found him half-delirious in the doorway, throwing his voice and making one very large crow seemingly squawk, "Nevermore!" The bird, obviously confused and flustered by the voice from its own throat, leapt about and squawked angrily back at Robert, who only laughed harder and kept repeating, "Nevermore! Nevermore!" Margaret was not so amused by his antics and had to yank the magician by his ears back into the warmth of the study.

Robert did not improve. Increasingly bored as the dour month wore on, he no longer tried to hide his habit of reading. A full collection of Shakespeare's works could often be found at his elbow as he dozed, drank, and immersed himself in the bard. Sherpa, who had come to watch over Rouncival as well, told both women he heard through closed doors the sound of many voices coming from all points, both high and low, within the study. One was old and cracked, another was a mocking lilt, while another was a crazed beggar. Curious, all three padded towards the study and put their ears to the doors. Shocked, the women realized Rouncival was enacting a scene from *King Lear*, with lampshades, couches, or what have you playing the parts of the mad King, his fool, and Tom O' Bedlam. Nora knocked softly, entered the study, and shut the inlaid doors behind her. The voices stopped.

The onset of winter did not. December arrived with a bluster and for a week the strong winds and clattering panes wreaked havoc with everyone's nerves. To ease their minds, Sherpa, Margaret, and Nora decorated the manor for the season. Garlands of holly were strung everywhere, though Robert in his distraction often snipped off the popcorn as a snack in passing. He refused to let anyone decorate the study, however, and grew cross if he heard even the slightest melody of a carol. He claimed it disturbed his recording of "Solace," which on some days he played almost continuously. Festive the manor was not.

Then the winds calmed and a bright, bright morning dawned. The air lost some of its chill and Robert ventured outside for the first time in a week. He quickly pronounced the afternoon splendid, returned to gather some blankets, and then went back out again to sit in a large, wooden lawn chair near the milepost beneath the oaks. With a packet of cigarettes in one pocket and his pipe in another, Rouncival sat amidst the fallen leaves, puffed his pipe, and cheerfully stared at nothing. Margaret took the opportunity and ventured into the study to do some quick picking up. That very night, she wrote to Silver.

A long day, a mysterious day, a day I shall never forget. Sunshine for the first time in ages, and not even a breeze, never mind the hurricane buffeting we've been getting, to spoil the thaw. Robert for once left his lair and sat out on the lawn, wrapped head to toe like a laird in motley, and I figured I could at least take the chance to remove some of the stacks of plates, glasses, and full ashtrays strewn throughout the study. Then thinking that I wanted to write you tonight but had no stamps, I checked to see that Robert wasn't looking, figuring even Robert has to have some stamps around. With the coast clear I snuck to that desk he stole from

Chekhov (I know, I know, Anton is long gone but that's always how I think of the thing) and began rifling the drawers. "If Robert catches me, I'll never hear the end of it," I thought as I tried to think up an excuse just in case. Lo and behold, he did have some stamps stashed away, though I think they've been around for about five years, and I checked again to see if he had seen me. He wasn't looking my way at all, but when I saw him, I caught my breath and slowly, slowly went to the window.

He was sitting like normal, in all those ridiculous tartan shawls and robes (I think every Highland clan is represented on Robert's back alone), staring up at the trees. A few scraggly leaves still hung from the limbs, but most were piled in equally tartan heaps all around him. But as I blinked and blinked again, the leaves seemed to rise, first in tiny, eddying swirls. I thought, "Oh no, the wind again, he'd better come inside," but then I noticed that nothing else, not so much as a twig or a blade of brown grass, was moving also. Everything but the leaves was still. Then I saw Robert's mouth moving slightly, and the leaves began to swirl even faster, rising as though they'd been caught in a whirlwind. They twisted and rose up towards the trees but no higher, circling Robert all the while, and then they began to spin downwards again. As some rose and others fell, all the leaves began to turn, and I mean turn colors. They were dark green again, then orange or crimson, then pale as spring blossoms, all winding and circling Robert. I could hardly breathe, all I heard was my heart pounding, and then I did hear something, a rising and falling refrain, and though Robert's mouth was moving it seemed to emanate and swell from the leaves. I pressed my face against the glass, and just barely I began to hear what they were saying. It was a part of a speech from Macbeth *but only a small part re-*

peated over and over as all of the leaves, flowing in and out of seasons, sang in the round, ". . . a poor player that struts and frets his hour upon the stage . . . it is a tale . . . a poor player . . ." All the words began to merge, the tale, the player, the fretting hours as the leaves sang in the round, rising, falling, suspended almost but still moving from spring to winter and back again. And as I kept holding my breath, I saw Robert in the center of it all, his mouth moving, reciting the passages for every leaf, every color, making the seasons rise and fall, and then for a moment, a moment so brief, a light seemed to swell from inside Robert himself, spinning and winding its way from the shawls, and he was young again. Oh how young he was, his face full and his eyes bright, and the circles and grays and pallor were all gone. Even the grass beneath his feet was green, and for a second I was green also, a dizzy debutante in thrall, looking for thrills and staring at the player on the stage, all cockiness, pride, and triumph, able to create life, anything he wanted to, myself or himself even, right out of thin air. It was too much, almost as if my heart had begun to beat backwards, and I closed my eyes against the feeling. When I opened them again a moment later, there was Robert, huddled in his shawls, and it was a December day again and the leaves were still and brown and fallen on the ground, and I heard him give a short laugh, "Hah!" and that was all.

Now, it is late, and I am so tired but I can't forget it. I can't get Robert out of my mind's eye. I see him there all the time, first young and then old, and I think that if he was a Hindu or belonged to some belief of any kind, Robert would choose to start over again as Robert every time, forever and ever. Perhaps it's his deepest fault, or maybe it's his greatest feat, but deep in his heart Robert is the only person I've ever known who's truly never desired to be anyone or anything other than himself.

Two days later, on December 12, Sherpa brought a pot of strong tea to Rouncival in the study. Robert was in the Khan's tent like always, and thanked Sherpa quietly. Sherpa, seeing he was tired, turned to leave, then heard Robert say, "Funny, my leg ..." When he looked back in concern, Sherpa saw Robert silhouetted at the window, seemingly okay and looking out at the lawns, one hand holding his cup, the other lightly touching the glass. Sherpa made to leave again, and as he shut the doors as softly as he could, he heard Robert murmur behind him, "Oh Doughboy, have I got one for you now." Sherpa returned an hour later to look in and found Rouncival collapsed on the carpet amidst the oriental pillows. He had suffered a second, and this time massive, stroke. Laying his head against Robert's chest, all Sherpa heard was the tick of Robert's watch.

Robert "The Great" Rouncival was buried in a place of honor beneath a Japanese maple in the Kaatershook cemetery. Despite many lifetimes worth of experience, he was only forty years old.

THE

Gloaming
Heir

Ladies and gentlemen, for all intents and purposes, that concludes the tour. While Robert Rouncival was often not a very good man, he was most certainly a great one. Before you take your leave, however, and I realize I have indeed kept you well into the twilight, I believe it is time to reveal a bit about myself. I am, in fact, the only son of Sherpa and Margaret. My full name is Juan Quixote Tillinghast Hernandez, and while I shall not burden your hearts with any more details of death, I will say that Rouncival willed the entirety of his estate, including the study, to my parents. Many, many years later, I in turn inherited it along with the majority of my mother's Wampum holdings. Perhaps fearing the Wampum curse myself, I quickly divested myself of all interest in that company, though I do remain one of the top shareholders in Blackwood Studios.

As for Bill Silver, he lived long past Rouncival's death as well. Eventually the Bowery became all too clean-cut for his tastes, and following the Second World War and the establishment of Israel, he moved to the country of his forefathers. Though my family, and then I, kept in touch with him for quite a while, he has since fallen from view. I know from certain matters regarding Blackwood Studios that his stock remains in his name, however, and he is in all likelihood still among the living. Always somewhat of a benefactor, always somewhat mysterious, Silver was long the subject of discussion in our household. In the end, we believe that it was no coincidence Robert mastered his first illusion of levitation, "The Wandering Jew," under the old man's roof at the Half-Shell Palace.

As for myself, I have been happily married for many years, and have been blessed with two, now grown twin sons. The older, by three minutes, is named Roberto, while his brother is called Robert. I can truly say there have been only two sorrows in my life: that my wife and I were never graced with a daughter who we would have named Evelyn Tillinghast Hernandez, and the fact that I am the last member of the Harbingers' Club. I would have liked to induct my sons, but by the time they had come of age there was no one else remaining to second the nominations. Should they desire so, it appears they will have to begin a society of their own.

Ladies and gentlemen, from the bottom of my heart, I thank you for coming. As we look the length of the study, from the cover of *Life* past the paper vaquero and all the way to the Khan's tent in the distance, it is both a lifetime and a day that we have spent together. A bit of trickery so mystifyingly simple Robert himself might have been proud of it. I do thank you again, and hope you have enjoyed your time here in the study of Robert the Great. Ladies and gentlemen, I hope you have enjoyed visiting *my* study. Good evening.

ACKNOWLEDGMENTS

I'd like to thank my mother, Hollis Rowan Seamon, for her excellent advice and accurate warning systems when I first began blathering about the misadventures of Robert and Sherpa. Her early suggestions and enthusiasm helped me avoid many pitfalls, and any ugly tumbles are entirely due to my own mulishness. Thanks also to Dennis Mahoney, for his constant e-encouragement as the project went from short fiction to I-don't-know-what-to-call-it-anymore-man. The good people of Spring Harbor need to be lauded, for their generosity of spirit and unflinching tips to an often-wayward traveler. Last but certainly not least, to my own little Harbingers' Club: Nicky, B., and always and always, to Gretchen.